The Seeing

Also by Diana Hendry

Harvey Angell
Harvey Angell and the Ghost Child
Harvey Angell Beats Time

The Awesome Bird
You Can't Kiss It Better

The Seeing

Diana Hendry

CORGI BOOKS

THE SEEING
A CORGI BOOK 978 0 552 56569 1

First published in Great Britain by The Bodley Head,
an imprint of Random House Children's Publishers UK
A Random House Group Company

The Bodley Head edition published 2012
This edition published 2013

3 5 7 9 10 8 6 4 2

Penguin Random House is committed to a sustainable future for our business, our readers and our planet. This book is made from Forest Stewardship Council® certified paper.

Printed and bound in Great Britain by Clays Ltd, St Ives plc

Set in Adobe Garamond Pro

Corgi Books are published by Random House Children's Publishers UK,
61–63 Uxbridge Road, London W5 5SA

www.**randomhousechildrens**.co.uk
www.**totallyrandombooks**.co.uk
www.**randomhouse**.co.uk

Addresses for companies within The Random House Group Limited can be found at:
www.randomhouse.co.uk/offices.htm

THE RANDOM HOUSE GROUP Limited Reg. No. 954009

A CIP catalogue record for this book is available from the British Library.

Contents

For Hamish II

Love . . . adds a precious seeing to the eye

Shakespeare, *Love's Labour's Lost*

Prologue

The pills don't help. It's been three weeks now and every night it's the same. I'm trying to stop it all happening and I can't. The fire's eating up the whole beach. Even the sea can't put it out, can't even reach it. It's as if the sea sees the flames streaking the sky in a hellish mix of red, orange, yellow – and draws back, afraid. Looking at it could blind you. Its roar terrifies. Some nights Lal and Paul are there in their wedding clothes, but somehow the fire can't touch them. They're immune. The flames seem to lick round Lal's white satin wedding dress without even singeing it like an iron might. And Lal simply lifts up her arms to dance with Paul. Sometimes it's Hugo and Philip I see. Hugo's carrying his easel. Philip's holding a bunch of paintbrushes like a bouquet. They're so busy talking they haven't even noticed the fire – or, if they have, they don't care. And I know they're in terrible danger but I can't speak. The smoke from the fire is choking me. Whether it's Lal and Paul in the fire or Hugo and Philip walking away from it, it always ends the same way – me screaming for Natalie.

Then Mum comes in and shakes me awake. She has to shake me, she says, because I'm like someone in a fever. So she shakes me and

I can hear her voice coming from a long way off, calling, 'Lizzie! Lizzie! Wake up, darling!' Waking is such a shock I'm immediately shivering with fright, and Mum grabs my dressing gown and wraps it round me. That's if I *do* wake up. Some mornings – and this is weird and awful – I'm awake but I'm still in the dream. The dream – the fire – is still blazing and I'm reaching out trying to save someone, only I don't know who.

I know even Mum is frightened when I'm like that. Once she dragged me out of bed and pulled me over to the mirror. 'Look!' she said. 'You're awake! It's morning! You've had a nightmare. Look at yourself!'

Only it wasn't me I saw in the mirror. It was Natalie. Then I knew that, of all the things Natalie had been wrong about, she was right about this. Evil doesn't just stop. However much good there is in the world, evil doesn't stop.

Mum cradled me in her arms then, and stroked my hair and said, 'It'll be all right, Lizzie. It will be all right.'

But I know it won't be all right. How can it be, without Natalie?

Chapter 1
Wild Spirit

Natalie blew into my life like the wild west wind of Shelley's poem which our English teacher read to us, letting her voice go into a crescendo with:

Wild Spirit, which art moving everywhere;
Destroyer and preserver; hear, oh hear!

She appeared in our class halfway through the summer term. I didn't know where she'd come from and I didn't care. I thought she was wonderful. I thought she was like no one else I'd ever met. She made Alice and Dottie – they've been my best friends since first year – look dull. It didn't matter that Natalie was wearing what we all recognized as a second-hand school uniform, she wore it like it was a challenge to someone or something. Her gymslip was a dare shorter than anyone else's. She wore the girdle slung low around her skinny hips and her tie – a kind of frayed rag you could just about recognize as being in the green and purple school colours – dragged to one side. No socks, just plimsolls, and her hair a wild mass of uncombed curls yanked up with a tatty scarlet ribbon. Everything about her, from her fierce brown eyes to the kind of strutting walk she had, gave off defiance, as if she knew who she was and no one was going to change her.

Perhaps that was what made her different from the rest of us. We were all finding out who we were. Sometimes I thought I was trying on selves like you try on clothes in a shop. Which self was really, really me? Natalie knew. On the day she arrived – and Miss Roberts told us all to welcome her and then took her aside and pointed to her feet so we knew she was suggesting socks – I looked at her and she reached to my heart. She went straight there, as if there was something in her that was in me too, only I hadn't known it before and though I didn't know what it was, I knew it was important. I wanted her for my friend like I'd never wanted anything before. Not even ballet lessons when I was seven! I had – what can I call it? – a kind of flash of recognition so that even though I hadn't said a word to her and she hadn't said a word to me, I kind of *knew* her. I knew her by heart as it were, like my mum can play the piano by heart – or by ear, without any music.

It was very obvious that this flash didn't go both ways. Natalie barely looked at me. And why should she? I knew what she'd see. A nice, well-behaved, good girl! A girl who was always tidy and neat. A girl often top of the class. A girl who wore expensive shoes and socks. How could she possibly see the matching wildness I felt inside me?

Not that Natalie seemed to want any friends. You'd think, being new, she'd make some effort, but she didn't. At break time she sat at the far end of the playing field, hunched up under the trees and scribbling in a small notebook. At lunch time she always found a seat by herself. She ate very fast. Everything. Even the worst sago puddings in the world. And then she was off out into the village –

which, strictly speaking, wasn't allowed, though nobody quite dared to tell on her. She could give you a look with those fierce brown eyes of hers that made you want to sink into the ground.

There was lots of gossip about who she was and where she'd come from.

'She comes from London,' Alice said.

'How d'you know?' I asked.

'She's got that look,' Alice told me. 'You know – that tough city look.'

I knew what she meant, even if a 'look' wasn't exactly proof. Natalie made the rest of us village kids look like – well, village kids.

'My mum says they're hiding out,' Alice continued.

'Hiding out? Who from?'

She shrugged. 'I don't know. Rent collectors, I think. Mum says they were evicted from their last place. That means thrown out.'

'I know what *evicted* means,' I said, irritated. 'How does your mum know all this?'

'Monty's,' said Alice. She didn't need to say any more. Monty's was the village coffee shop. Correction. The village *gossip* shop.

'*And*,' she added, as if she now had the final piece of news, 'she doesn't have a dad.'

'I shall pray for her,' said Dottie. Dottie has recently got Jesus. She went to a big meeting in town and heard this American evangelist called Billy Graham and got saved. Now she wants to save everyone else. She walks around with a Bible and gives me little prayer cards. I think she's given up fun.

'I doubt she'll thank you for it,' Alice said sharply (she's a bit fed up with Dottie too).

'I don't expect thanks,' Dottie said, and stalked off as if we'd offended her.

Actually, although as far as we knew Natalie didn't have a dad, what we knew she *did* have was a little brother.

Philip was at the primary school and there was something wrong with him. He wore thick pebble specs, walked with a limp and stuttered. When Amanda Newton called Philip 'loopy', Natalie slapped her face. It happened in the playground and caused an impressed silence. I half expected Dottie to drop to her knees then and there.

Philip always waited for Natalie at the school gate so that they could walk home together. Somehow that made the rest of us keep away from her. She acted as if she didn't care. Walked away whistling, Philip dragging behind her.

I don't think Natalie would ever have noticed me if it hadn't been for Philip, and if I hadn't been at the swimming pool on the afternoon when he fell in the deep end. I was there just at the right moment to jump in and haul him out.

It's always been a mystery to me why we have a swimming pool in Norton when we have the sea. In fact, the swimming pool's next door to the sea! You can come out by the turnstile past the woman who sells you a ticket, and go straight onto the beach. Maybe they built The Baths (as we call it) because sea people need to swim at all hours of the day and night and you can't count on the tide being in. Or maybe it was the Council's way of making money or they thought the sea was dangerous – which it is at times – or just because someone thought it would be nice.

Whoever built The Baths must have been living in some kind of Eastern dream because the place looks as if it landed in Norton after being flown here from Arabia on a magic carpet. It has fat, white, lumpy walls (like pretend mud, whitewashed) with a dome at each corner. Inside there are fountains, bubbling over onto coloured stones. There's a sunbathing terrace, a choice of slides from Little to Curly to Steep, and a café where you can buy hot chocolate.

I'd never have been at The Baths that afternoon if it hadn't been for Mum. I was curled up on the sofa reading a book when she appeared, handing me my swimming costume Swiss-rolled into a towel.

'Maybe you haven't noticed,' she said, 'but it's sunny out there. Go and get some fresh air.'

I went. Grumbling. As soon as I was in I spotted Natalie and Philip. Natalie was on the sunbathing terrace, lying on her tummy and scribbling in that notebook that seemed to go everywhere with her. Philip was wandering about in his underpants, sometimes taking his specs off and holding them up to the sun as if there was something not quite right with them which the sun might make better.

I don't think the boy meant to push him in the deep end. I think he was just rushing past and Philip was too near the edge and neither quick nor steady on his feet. He went in with a howl. His specs floated to the surface as he bobbed up and down, up and down, his arms thrashing, his mouth still open in the howl, only now there was no sound coming out of it. Then Natalie was there, screaming at me, 'I can't swim! I can't swim!' And I know I shouldn't have let such a selfish thought cross my mind, but it did. *Well, she's noticed me now*, I thought. Then I dived in.

I learned to swim when I was six. I can't imagine *not* being able to swim. Philip was light. It was easy to grab him and drag him to the bar where he clung on, spluttering and gasping until Natalie reached down, got him under the arms and hauled him out. I even managed to rescue Philip's specs.

'Thanks,' Natalie said casually, as if I hadn't just saved Philip's life.

'Thanks,' over her shoulder while thumping him on the back until he coughed up half the swimming pool and his colour – such as it was – came back. Then she walked away.

That's it, I thought. She'll ignore me again tomorrow. But she didn't. She was waiting for me outside school.

'Let's go down to the pier,' she said as if we'd already agreed to meet.

A twice life-size picture of the pier loomed into my head. The pier. Dangerous. Great open slats you could almost drop through. Rotting ones that could give way under you. *Death by drowning*, I thought, unless the lifeboat got to us in time, that is. And there was Mum. I don't know if all mothers can do this, but mine has the knack of speaking to me when she isn't there. I mean I can hear her voice in my head, and what she said right now was *Don't go off the beaten track!* I knew she'd be expecting me home, probably watching out for me from the top front bedroom. I switched her off. Natalie was waiting. One hand on her hip, the other holding Philip. There was a kind of take-it-or-leave-it challenge on her face.

'OK,' I said, as casually as if daring rotten piers was something I did every day of the week. 'Let's go.'

Natalie's Diary

Sunday

Philip nearly drowned yesterday. A girl from my class jumped in and saved him. Lizzie. That's her name. She lives in one of those big houses at the other end of the village. Must be rich. We might need funds for the New Plan. Would she do? She looks sort of sweet-but-interesting. And innocent. No one would suspect her.

NB to Self. Can't do this on my own. I must have someone!

I hate it here. Miss Roberts says Norton's quiet and peaceful.

I hate quiet and peaceful.

Quiet and peaceful means half asleep.

Quiet and peaceful means pretending everything's all right when it isn't.

Quiet and peaceful lets badness in.

But the sea's good. Sea's *never* quiet and peaceful.

NB to Self. Be sure to test Lizzie out first.

That's what they did in the Resistance Movement before they enlisted anyone. Tested them out. I got Lizzie to walk to the end of that rotten pier. She was dead scared – went white as a sheet – but she did it. And she doesn't laugh at Philip like some of them do. The ignorant ones.

Philip not settled. Hates new places. What's happened to his dreams? He hasn't had a decent one since we got here. Has he left his dreams in London? It's as if he's not quite here yet. Keeps waking up at night. Keeps crying.

Says he can't see properly. Ma says to tell him to shut up. *It's bloody dark. Course he can't see properly.* Much she knows! Much she understands! No one does.

Could I tell Lizzie? Don't know. Too early to tell. I don't know how serious a person she is. There aren't many really *serious* people about.

NB to Self. Don't trust too soon.

The men have started coming again. It's going to be the same as it was in London.

Chapter 2
Seeing Things

There's a notice at the foot of the pier. It says: KEEP OFF! DANGER!

The pier is a bit like The Baths, someone's dream. Mum says it was built before the war when people thought Norton would become a seaside holiday resort. It was going to be lit up. It was going to have a theatre and side booths selling candyfloss and stuff, and a Punch and Judy show. Then the war came and nothing was lit up and any plans for the pier were abandoned.

'What about afterwards?' I asked Mum.

'Everyone had gone off the idea,' she said. 'No one wanted rowdy day trippers coming over from town and making the place cheap. Kids on the beach in their knickers. Not nice.'

Mum's got notions about what's nice and what's not nice. Anyone would think that kids on the beach in their not-nice knickers is the worst thing that could happen to Norton.

Natalie gave the KEEP OFF! DANGER! the briefest look. Then she shrugged, gave me a grin, rolled up the sleeves of her shirt, took off her plimsolls and dumped them on the beach with her school bag. I did the same. I was still hoping she'd change her mind. Philip obviously felt the same way because he kept saying, 'Home now . . . H-h-h-home now.' Natalie ignored him.

The wind was just strong enough to make the sea leap up through the struts of the pier like the tongues of so many hungry dogs. My arms came out in goose bumps. Philip sat down in the sand and wouldn't budge.

'Leave him,' said Natalie. 'He'll be all right.' She was first up on the pier. I scrambled after. Once up there, somehow everything changed. There was just Natalie and me high above the sea, high above Norton, braving the wind, daring the rotten or missing slats, trying to hold steady and shrieking with laughter when we couldn't.

Looking back, I could see the tall houses that lined the prom like so many snooty aunts, and Philip, just a small figure now, standing up with his mouth wide open. He could have been screaming but the sound was lost in the wind. Further down the beach, tucked in along the slipway, was the artist's yellow caravan.

The artist has been coming to Norton every year since I can remember. Mum always says that you know summer's begun when the artist arrives. I thought he'd turned up that day like a good omen. It seemed perfect to see his caravan – from up on the pier it was just a splodge of bright yellow – on the first day Natalie and I were together, hanging onto each other, the wind blowing my hair over my eyes, turning Natalie's scarlet ribbon into a streamer. *It's not just the start of summer,* I thought. *It's the start of my life. My life proper now I'm almost fourteen, now I've met Natalie.*

At the far end of the pier we sat down close to each other, cold arms touching, legs dangling over the edge. It was as near to being out at sea as you could get without a boat. Natalie began mimicking the seagulls and soon we were both screeching our heads off and laughing so hard it's a wonder we didn't fall off.

What was I expecting, hoping for? It was too vague for me to name. Excitement, I suppose. Adventure. Risk. Someone who'd help me escape from my dull home life. Someone I could speak my heart to. Someone I could tell how guilty I felt about not wanting peace when everyone else, everyone who'd been through the war, was really glad of it.

When we walked back down the pier, Natalie and me, I wanted to say something like 'friends for ever'. It crossed my mind how people in stories cut their hands and rub the blood together. Somehow I didn't think that was Natalie's style. Anyway, I missed my moment because as we neared the beach, Philip's yells came alive.

'Not safe! Not safe!' he was wailing.

'Philip can see things,' Natalie said.

'What sort of things?'

'Things other people can't,' she said. Then she wouldn't say any more.

I looked at Philip more carefully then. We were back on the beach and Natalie was busy comforting him, wiping his face with the edge of her shirt, crooning at him, putting his shoes on, his specs. Those specs! The ones I'd managed to grab out of the swimming pool. The lenses were as thick as the bottom of milk bottles. And without his specs I'd guess the whole world was a blur. My dad has specs with thick lenses. When he takes them off, he blinks at me like an owl in daylight. Without his specs he can just about tell the difference between my sister Lal and me, and that's only because she's about five inches taller.

So what could Natalie mean when she said Philip could see things other people couldn't? Maybe he can see in the dark! Lal told me once that because blind people can't see, their other senses become much sharper – something like Beethoven being deaf but able to hear music in his head. Maybe Philip has that extra-sensory something or other. I looked at him sitting there in the sand, his face all bleary from crying, and doubted that he had an extra anything.

Natalie was different now that we were off the pier. It was as if she'd lost interest in me and it was just the dare that mattered.

'Got to go,' she said, gathering up her things. 'We've got work to do.'

'Work? What work? What d'you mean?'

Natalie didn't answer. She was off up the beach, Philip trailing after.

'See you tomorrow!' I called, but she barely turned her head.

I went off home. The excitement was draining out of me. Was this how it was going to be with Natalie? One moment she felt close as close, the next moment she was all distant.

It's only a five-minute walk from the pier to our house, but lately every time I'm on my way home I get a kind of tummy ache. It's as if I don't want to go there. It's as if home isn't home any more. I don't quite know how it's happened. It might have begun last year when Dad got a new car, had the whole house painted and bought new carpets and thick velvet curtains and a television that's hidden inside a cupboard. Mum keeps talking about 'going up in the world', and sometimes she puts on what she thinks is a posh accent and tries not to laugh too loudly.

I think it's something to do with the prime minister saying that we've never had it so good. When I asked Mum what he meant, she just said, 'Oh, Lizzie, you were a war baby, you don't remember how dreadful life was then. You're very, very lucky to be growing up in a time of peace.'

That's what she's always saying, that I'm lucky to be growing up in a time of peace. I want to tell her – I want to tell everyone – that it doesn't *feel* lucky. It feels like turning up when history's stopped and you've missed all the action and what you're left with is boring old peace. But that's just not the kind of thing you can say out loud. It would be like saying the world was square or God never existed or children shouldn't go to school.

When I tried to tell Lal that I thought peace was boring, she blew up at me. 'Never say that again!' she said. 'Don't you know that millions of people died?'

And then I felt very guilty because of course I knew that millions of people had died and I knew about Hitler and I knew about the concentration camps and how awful our life would be if we hadn't won the war. Only I couldn't help feeling that at least during the war you had something to fight for, while peace left you nothing. If our house was anything to go by, peace was about buying things and making money and 'going up in the world', and having cream with your apple pie and net curtains under the thick velvet ones and being respectable and nice and dull, dull, dull.

It was daft, but somehow the plush new carpets that kept out all the draughts and the heavy velvet curtains that kept out even a chink of light made me feel as if I was shut off from the world. I hated it that Dad had a new lock put on the front door when we always used to leave it open as if to say that everyone was welcome.

When Alice came round I could tell she was jealous, particularly of the new television in its special cupboard. When Dottie came for tea, she looked about her, and in her most preachy voice she said, 'It is easier for a camel to go through the eye of a needle than for a rich man to enter into the kingdom of God.' Then she sat down in front of the television and hogged the biscuits.

I missed our house as it used to be, with the front door always open and just a few rugs on the floors and nobody minding if I drew on the wall in the dining room and the stairs having a special creak on the ninth step and sunlight and moonlight allowed in. Oh – and a few draughts.

And I missed Lal, Lal as she was before she fell in love with Paul. Before Paul there was something really grand about my sister. She's tall, dark and dramatic looking – or at least she *was*. I'd see her setting off to work on the top deck of the double-decker like Boadicea setting forth, the warrior queen in her scarlet and blacks. Now she's all lilac and pink and it's as if love has taken the stiffening out of her. Some days she's even quite nice to me. I liked it better when she shut her bedroom door in my face or, out in the garden, whipped my legs with nettles. Paul's a sailor and Lal's going to marry him. The wedding's to be in September. Lal spends all her time writing letters to him on that thin airmail paper or talking about the wedding to her friends on the phone. Or moping. Sometimes I find myself wishing that Paul wouldn't come back from sea so that Lal could be mine again, a proper sister sharing things like we used to do. I don't want Paul dead or drowned or anything, maybe just lost in another country. China or Australia. Then forgetting to come back. There's still time before September for Paul to get lost or Lal to change her mind. I don't want to think about the time when she leaves home, even though it means I get her bedroom, which is the best one because it looks out over the garden.

I thought maybe I could tell Lal about Natalie. About walking the pier. But then I thought not. Somehow I felt Natalie was a secret I didn't want to share with anyone just yet. I certainly wasn't going to tell Mum.

She was waiting for me at the front door, white-faced and angry.

'Where have you been? Where have you been?' she demanded and slapped my face.

'A detention,' I lied.

Actually the slap was almost a relief. Mum's been so preoccupied with Lal's wedding it was a wonder she'd missed me at all. The slap was more like things being as they usually were – that is, Mum having one of her worry attacks. The list of things Mum worries about could fill a book. Crossing the road. Going off the beaten track. Talking to strange men. Accepting a lift from a stranger. Going out without a vest. Going out with my hair wet. Just going out. Well, that's some of them. One way or another, as far as Mum's concerned, I'm in constant danger. I think it's because Mum is Jewish but my dad isn't. Mum 'married out'. That's what they call it when a Jewish person marries a non-Jewish person.

And because she married out she was cut off from all her relatives, brothers, sisters, aunts, uncles . . . She was sort of dead to them. I've worked out that Mum thinks God is angry with her for doing this and likely to punish her by getting at us, Lal and me. Mum believes in the Old Testament God. He's bigger and angrier and more jealous than the New Testament one – at least that's what Dottie says, and she should know. I think she's read both. Twice.

Mum hasn't exactly told me any of this and most of the time, when she's out and about, shopping in her best dress or cooking Sunday lunch, you'd never guess how she is when she falls asleep by the fire on a winter afternoon. How she groans! Awful deep groans as if that angry Old Testament God was just behind her or ready to throw one of His thunderbolts. I think He has thunderbolts.

Once she'd slapped me, Mum hugged me and gave me a long nag about not having any note from school about a detention, and in any case, what had I done wrong to get a detention in the first place? And she'd had tea ready and now it was ruined, and so on and on and on. Luckily she was too cross to wait for any answers so I could escape to my room.

I flopped on my bed feeling miserable, feeling I'd been born into the wrong family and really Natalie should be my sister. No, maybe my twin! I got up and tried back-combing my hair so that it looked vaguely curly, but it wouldn't stay that way. I did what I often do when I'm upset, I got out my drawing pad. I tried drawing a picture of Natalie. It didn't look very like her, perhaps because I drew her smiling and when I thought about it, Natalie didn't smile much.

Drawing made me think of the artist in his yellow caravan. I wondered if he was happy being on his own, just drawing and painting, or if he got lonely. Perhaps this year I could draw something good enough to show him – that is if it wasn't breaking Mum's rule about not talking to strange men. How many years did he have to come to Norton before he wasn't regarded as a stranger?

I put the drawing of Natalie under my pillow so no one would see it and also because putting it there felt like a wish. A wish that from now on she'd be my best friend. That tomorrow she wouldn't ignore me.

Lal says you should be careful what you wish for because it might come true.

She was right.

The Caravan
Early morning

Dear Helena,
Just to let you know I've arrived, and to make me feel at home I've been woken up by seagulls. I know, I know, they're terribly noisy and squawky and you hate them, but I love them. They always sound as if they've been told something very urgent by the sea and now they're off to tell all their friends and relatives.

The caravan needs some attention. It felt a bit damp when I arrived, and I'll try and give it a coat of paint sometime during this summer. Do you know this is my eighth summer here? Well, eight not counting that one day's holiday when we were brought here as children. I think it must have been one of the few times we were allowed to be together and that was only because the Terrible Sisters fancied an outing. I think you'd almost forgotten you had a brother. You must have been, what . . . seven? I was ten and I looked at this beach and the sea, the sea stretching out to the islands and beyond and I said to Aunty Em (as she made me call her, remember?), 'I don't want to go back to your house.' And she clipped me over the ear and told me I was an ungrateful brat. That made you cry.

Well, I've four whole months here just drawing and painting and looking. Odd how looking sounds easy and is really the hardest. Probably only you know how much I need this place. How it helps me look at some of those bad war memories safely, without getting ill. I think it's the light and the space and the way the sea rolls itself back into the sky so you can't tell one from the other. It puts those dark memories into the light. Your Derek once told me that he remembered having measles as a child, and when he was better his mum put all the bedclothes and pyjamas and things out in the sunshine to get rid of all the infection. It's something like that. I can hear you tutting a bit and saying that I must stop looking into the past and start painting what's new. So that's what I'm going to do and it's going to be children. Children on a beach.

I hope you'll be pleased because I've got some in mind. Spotted them yesterday. They're a trio. Two girls about thirteen or so, and a boy, much younger. I saw the girls daring the pier. Remember that pier? They should have pulled it down years ago. Either that or mended it. It looks even worse this year. At least they've put up a sign saying DANGER! KEEP OFF! *You know, in my opinion, there's some people who just love the word* danger. *They're drawn to it like it was a magnet. I could tell one of the girls, the dark-haired one, was just like that. Even from a distance I could see it in her walk, that sort of defiance in the shoulders, the toss of the hair. I could be wrong, of course. Maybe she's a real sweetie and not the wild child I took her for. Sometimes it's hard to know the difference between seeing and imagining.*

I kept a close eye on my trio in case I had to make a dash to call out the coastguard or the police. Perhaps I should have done that right away. Perhaps there's that same love of danger, of risk, in me – I know you'd say there was. Well, I didn't call anyone. I just kept watch.

To begin with the second girl looked a bit uncertain about walking on the pier. I thought, She's the dreamy one – doesn't look where she's going. I thought she was going to put her foot through a hole in the slats at any moment. But she got better at it. By the time they were sitting at the end of the pier they might well have been friends for life, perched there, arms round each other. I couldn't hear them, but I knew they were laughing.

Actually it was the boy I was most worried about. They left him sitting in the sand and howling. He was a scruffy wee lad. Looked as if no one had combed his hair for a week or two. Or possibly fed him, he was that skinny. If I hadn't thought it would scare him silly – or worse, make the girls run back to him along that unsafe pier – I'd have gone over to comfort him.

I watched until I saw the girls were back safe on the beach. I did a quick sketch of them – just outlines really. I know what you're thinking. That I'd have done better to go over and give them a lecture about dangerous piers rather than making a sketch. It's that old dilemma, isn't it? Art or action.

Well, I think I've found my subjects for this summer. Two girls and a boy.

Love to Derek and lots to you,
Hugo

Chapter 3
Kin

The next day it was as if we had cut our hands and rubbed bloods together. I'd hardly hung up my blazer and changed into my pumps when Natalie claimed me.

'I've bagged our desks for history,' she said, drawing me away from Alice and Dottie.

I could see Alice raising her eyebrows and Dottie pulling a face. I mouthed 'Sorry' at them.

And that's how it was for the rest of the day. Instead of spending break time with Alice and Dottie as I usually do, I was down the far end of the field with Natalie.

'You don't need them,' she said. 'They're just boring. You're different. You've got . . .' She paused, and I hung on, waiting for her to tell me what I had that was different from anyone else.

'Nerve,' Natalie said. 'Courage.'

I felt nerve and courage grow in me as she spoke. That's what she could do to you, Natalie – fire you up.

'You and me,' she said, 'we're together, right?'

'Right!' I said.

So that's mostly how it was for the rest of that term.

Being 'together' with Natalie wasn't easy. It wasn't like having a gossip and a laugh with Alice or an argument about God with Dottie. Being with Natalie was somehow serious. Serious and exciting. Natalie was always hinting that there was something we were going to do that was important, that she'd tell me about when she was ready, that part of it depended on Philip.

I couldn't imagine *anything* depending on Philip. He was always waiting for us at the end of afternoon school, sometimes swinging on the gate and singing to himself. Natalie would grab hold of him and give him a little shake as if bringing him back to earth.

Most days I was late home now and when Mum wanted to know why, I told her that I had a new friend who had a little brother we needed to look after. It made Natalie sound all sweet and kind.

'What's this new friend's name?' Mum asked.

'Natalie,' I said.

'Ask her round,' Mum said. 'She could come for tea with Alice.'

But I didn't ask her round. There was something unmistakably wild about Natalie that every grown-up seemed to spot. It was like the difference between a wild cat and a pet. I'd seen how teachers at school reacted warily to her.

'Highly strung,' I'd overheard one teacher say. 'She could snap at any minute.'

I wasn't going to risk Mum recognizing that wildness. What might she do? Ban me from seeing Natalie? Decide to visit Natalie's mother? It didn't bear thinking about. And that was only part of it . . .

I knew Natalie lived on the council estate at the other end of the village. I knew from the clothes she wore – the second-hand (or third-hand) school uniform, Philip's old jersey with holes in the elbows – that there wasn't much money in her house. I remembered what Alice had said about Natalie and her mother being evicted from their last house and about Natalie not having a dad. I didn't like to ask her if any of that was true, but one way or another the thought of asking Natalie to my house made me feel embarrassed. I imagined her looking at the furniture – the three-piece suite in the sitting room, the sheepskin rug, the new television. Either she'd sneer or she'd be jealous. One or the other. I didn't want to find out which.

So I didn't invite her to my house and she didn't invite me to hers. We met up on the way to school. We sat together in class. At break we kept away from everyone else and sat at the far end of the field. It was always rather damp down there under the trees, but I didn't care. I was with Natalie.

I started wearing my uniform like she did, the gymslip girdle slung low round my hips, the tie a bit squiff, no socks.

'You'll be twins soon,' Alice said.

'What's it to you?' I asked. I was beginning to talk like Natalie.

'Nothing at all,' said Alice. 'If you can drop your real friends just like that, see if I care.'

I knew she did. I could see she had to turn away so I didn't see the tears in her eyes.

'Me and Natalie,' I called after her, 'we're kindred spirits.'

'Kindred nutters more like!' she said over her shoulder as she walked away.

I hadn't meant to tell Alice. It was what Natalie said a few days after we'd dared the pier. 'We're kin, you and me, kindred spirits,' she said.

The phrase sent a kind of thrill through me. I squeezed her arm and echoed it back. 'Kindred spirits, yes!'

Then we raced up the beach, Philip limping after us and calling, 'Wait! Wait!'

Most days we took to skipping school dinners and going to the fish and chip shop in Market Street. Natalie never had any money but I usually had enough to buy us both a large bag of chips and sometimes a sausage each. Once Natalie wrapped her sausage in a bit of paper and said she'd give it to Philip later. I felt so bad about this that the next time I had enough to buy sausages, I bought three. It meant I was a bit short of money for adding to my art box, but I didn't mind.

We were just slipping out one day – you had to do it while whichever teacher was on duty was watching the queue going into the dining hall – when Dottie appeared out of nowhere. She was standing at the gate, waiting for us and holding one of her prayer cards. She gave it to Natalie.

'I thought you might find this helpful,' she said. 'Sorry if I'm interrupting, Lizzie,' and she was off.

'What's this about?' Natalie asked.

'Dottie's been saved,' I said. 'She's got Jesus.'

'She's got a screw loose,' Natalie said, scrunching up the card and dropping it in the gutter, though not before I'd had time to read the start of it. *What a friend you have in Jesus* . . . it began.

'The thing is,' said Natalie when we'd found a place – just up from the artist's caravan – to sit and eat our chips, 'Jesus never really saved anyone.'

Of course I don't believe in the way Dottie believes, but I was a bit shocked by that. Also, although I think Dottie's, well, dotty, I'm fond of her. 'What d'you mean?' I asked.

'Well,' said Natalie, 'people die in fires or they drown at sea. Jesus doesn't save them.'

'I think Dottie means that he saves your soul,' I said.

'Oh, your soul,' said Natalie, tossing a chip to a passing seagull, 'a lot of use that is. Is that man watching us?'

'It's just the artist,' I said. 'He's here every summer.'

'He looks suspicious!' Natalie said.

I laughed. 'You sound like my mum,' I said. 'Any minute now you'll be telling me not to talk to strange men.'

Natalie didn't laugh back. 'You don't understand yet,' she said.

'Understand what?'

Natalie hesitated. I knew she'd been testing me. Daring the pier, skipping school at lunch time, even leaving my socks off had been a kind of test.

'When they tell you it's school rules to wear socks, you just say "Yes, miss," and carry on not wearing them,' Natalie said. 'They get tired of telling you after a while. You just don't give in.'

That's what I liked about Natalie – that not giving in, though I'd no idea then just how far she'd go, how much she'd risk once she got something fixed in her head.

Actually remembering *not* to wear socks was a pain. I had to take them off after I left the house, stuff them in my pocket and then remember to put them on again before I got home.

'Understand what?' I asked again.

'What's happening,' Natalie said.

I laughed. There we were on the beach in Norton with no one around except for one waggy dog and its man, plus an artist in a yellow caravan. The tide was far out. The houses along the front seemed to stand to attention. The sky was a soft, clear blue with only a few wispy clouds and the occasional chip-hunting seagull.

'I suppose you're used to life in London,' I said. 'This is Norton, peaceful little Norton, in boring, boring peace time. Nothing's happening. Nothing ever does happen here.'

Natalie didn't laugh. She looked at me pityingly. 'You just believe what you're told, don't you?' she said. 'Someone's told you it's peace time and you believe them.'

'Well, of course it's peace time,' I said. I felt quite cross with her and I hated that pitying look she gave me as if I was dumb or stupid. 'Everyone knows we won the war.'

'*Everyone knows!*' Natalie mocked. 'When are you going to start thinking for yourself?'

'This is stupid,' I said. 'I'm going back to school.'

'Please yourself,' said Natalie.

I was hoping she'd follow me, but she didn't. I made myself carry on without turning round. I went the other way back to the school road, back past the artist's caravan. As I got nearer I could hear jazz and see the artist sitting on the caravan's step. It looked as if he was sorting out his brushes. The music made me smile – it was as cheery as the caravan's yellow. It was foot-tapping summer music. I had the daft notion that it would be nice to stop and share the music with him. Seeing him sitting there in his familiar long shorts and paint-spattered shirt, his red hair almost fiery in the sunshine, I suddenly realized that he was handsome and that I'd never seen this before. The realization made me blush. *I'll say hello*, I thought and prepared my face. But just as I got close, the artist stood up, went inside the caravan and shut the door. I walked on and said hello to the waggy dog instead. It bounded off after its owner.

I hung about in the playground waiting for Natalie, not sure how she'd be, if she was still angry and mocking. She acted as if we hadn't fallen out at all. We linked arms and went back into the classroom.

'Kindred spirits for ever,' Natalie said.

'For ever,' I said, and felt a wave of relief.

I couldn't help but remember how easy things had been when Alice was my best friend and Dottie a kind of close second. When I was with Alice or Dottie I didn't have that sense of something really scary about to happen, or that either of them would ask me to do something really dangerous. But then there wasn't any excitement with Alice and Dottie, just every day being much the same. And Alice and Dottie didn't make me think about who I was or who I might be, as Natalie did. When I tried to think what was really different about Natalie, I realized it was that she had some kind of purpose, that her whole intense, skinny self was going to squeeze what she wanted out of life, come what may.

She wouldn't let the subject of peace go.

'I suppose you think you're safe here,' she said one afternoon after school when we'd gone back to the swimming pool with Philip. It was one of Philip's loopiest days when he babbled away to himself so that I remembered Natalie saying, *Philip can see things*, and wondered if he was seeing ghosts and talking to them. Philip either babbled or wouldn't speak for hours.

'Well,' I said, looking about The Baths at people swimming or sunbathing or reading or talking, 'I don't see anyone with a gun or a knife. There's no one shouting, *Your money or your life!* – not that I've got any money – so, yes, I suppose I do feel safe. Even though Mum seems to see danger round every corner.'

We were sunbathing on the terrace. I'd been for a swim while Natalie scribbled in her black book and Philip carried on talking to himself. I was drying myself and feeling happy. I didn't really want to talk about being safe. I was hoping that Natalie would suggest – well, maybe some kind of quest or adventure, something we could do together during the school holidays. Natalie had put her book down and was sitting up, watching me.

She seemed to be seriously considering the *money-or-your-life* option, as if there was a masked highwayman on his horse waiting for us outside The Baths.

'Of course it could be your money,' she said. 'You've got enough of it, haven't you?'

I felt myself going red. I hadn't wanted her to know about our house or about the big wedding Lal and my parents were planning. I shrugged.

'Or it could be your life,' Natalie continued. 'Or what about your country?'

'Anyone would think the war wasn't over, the way you go on,' I said, irritated again.

'And I suppose you think the war ends and everyone becomes good and kind.'

'Well . . .' I began.

Natalie didn't wait for an answer. She was sitting bolt upright now. She'd tied her hair up, but it was impossible to control the twisting curls that kept escaping from the band she'd used.

'How can evil just stop?' Natalie asked. Her dark brown eyes fixed on me intently. 'How can it?' she persisted. 'How can evil just stop?'

It was a warm June afternoon, almost muggy enough to make you sleepy, but Natalie's question made me shiver and pull my towel round me. It was the word 'evil' that did it. The word seemed to hover in the air between us, dark and bat-like. It was hardly out of Natalie's mouth when Philip began screaming.

He stood at the edge of the pool as if he had no idea he was on the edge and could topple in at any moment. He seemed to be staring at something or someone on the far side of the pool, though there was no one there and his hands were up as if someone was pointing a gun at him.

Natalie was on her feet in a flash. She grabbed hold of him, turning him so that his arms were round her waist and his face was buried in her T-shirt. The screams that had swimmers and sunbathers staring at him turned into sobbing and the sobbing into hiccups and the hiccups into silence.

One of the pool attendants was walking towards us.

'Is the lad all right?' he asked. He was a middle-aged man, sunburned from all the time he spent outside. Kindly. He knelt down and tried to look at Philip, but Natalie stood in the way.

'It sounded as if he'd really hurt himself,' the attendant said.

'He's fine!' Natalie said curtly. And to me, 'Let's go and get a hot chocolate from the café.'

'That should cheer him up,' the man said.

Natalie ignored him and began packing up their things.

The attendant gave up.

Philip liked it in the café (I paid for the hot chocolates, of course). He wandered from table to table pinching sugar lumps.

'What was he screaming at?' I asked. 'He looked as if he was staring at someone. Someone who wasn't there.'

Natalie sighed. 'I've told you,' she said. 'Philip can see things. Things other people can't see.'

'What d'you mean? Does he see ghosts? Can he see the future?'

Natalie leaned forward, elbows on the table, her hands reaching for mine. 'Listen,' she said. 'You're not to tell anyone this. Ever. Promise?'

'Course I promise,' I said.

'Philip has a gift,' Natalie said. 'He's got second sight.'

'So he *can* see the future,' I said.

'Sort of,' Natalie said. 'It's a gift that comes and goes. Philip's too young to control it yet. Sometimes it takes him over.'

'He started screaming when you began talking about evil,' I said. Somehow the word 'evil' even *tasted* nasty.

Natalie let go of my hands, sat back in her chair and allowed her eyes to idle around the café as if she'd got nothing better to do than examine the pictures of puffins and penguins on the walls.

'Who knows what he saw to make him scream like that,' she said – as if she knew exactly what it was but wasn't going to tell. 'Maybe it *was* something evil.'

There are some things that even a hot chocolate doesn't make better.

Philip wandered back to our table. He was humming to himself now. He looked as if he'd completely forgotten whatever it was he'd seen.

Chapter 4
Off the Beaten Track

I slept really badly that night. Or rather, I had a really bad night *not* sleeping. Natalie's question, *How can evil just stop?* kept repeating itself in my head as if it was going to go on repeating itself until I found an answer. I tossed and turned and I couldn't find one. A picture of Philip and how strange he looked standing on the edge of the swimming pool, staring at something or someone that neither Natalie nor I could see and screaming, flashed in the dark like someone shining a torch on a painting.

Had Philip seen something evil as Natalie had suggested? I didn't know whether to believe her or not. I half suspected it was another of her tests. Not the physical ones, like walking the pier or skipping school dinner, but some kind of mind test. I wished now I hadn't promised not to tell anyone about Philip's 'gift'. And anyway, was it a gift? Didn't he just need a doctor, or a head doctor, a psychiatrist?

One way or another, Mum couldn't have chosen a worse Saturday to tell me we were going into town to look at wedding dresses and bridesmaids' dresses.

'Do we have to?' I said. 'The wedding's months away. It might never happen.'

‘Of course it’s going to happen,’ Mum snapped.

Lal was deep in a letter from Paul. My sister’s been sitting opposite me at breakfast ever since I can remember. I wondered how it would be when she was gone and I’d just be looking at her empty chair, like she was dead. That made me feel so miserable it put me off my toast.

Lal folded up the letter and put it back in its envelope. ‘Is it too much to ask to have a *happy* bridesmaid?’ she asked. ‘Lots of girls really *want* to be a bridesmaid.’

‘I don’t see why it’s got to be such a showy wedding,’ I said. ‘It’s so embarrassing!’ I was thinking of our pictures in the local *Advertiser* and the way everyone in Norton stops to watch a wedding and how Natalie would see me and mock.

‘What’s the point of a wedding if it’s *not* showy?’ Mum said. ‘We’re *showing* how happy we are.’

‘And how much money we’ve got,’ I said.

‘Oh, give over!’ Mum said.

She took us to the bridal department of Cripps. Cripps is the biggest and grandest shop in town. Its name runs across the front in chunky gold letters, and when you go in there’s a carpeted hush, almost as if you’re in a church. The shop assistants don’t quite bow, but they all look at you as if you’re the next best thing to royalty. All of them, that is, except for the one we got in the bridal department. She was so smart and sophisticated in her black suit and her hair lacquered into a stiff bun that it almost felt rude to bother her. BABS, it said on the brooch pinned to the lapel of her suit.

Babs kept calling Mum ‘Modom’ but in a very weary voice as if it pained her to serve customers like us, as if we were the wrong class of people.

'Does Modom have an account?' Babs asked.

Mum was looking all bright and jaunty. She'd put on her best flowery dress that she kept for going into town and her new navy leather handbag in which was the new cheque book that Dad had given her.

'I shall be paying by cheque,' Mum said loftily.

Lal winked at me. It was obvious Mum wasn't going to let Babs put her down.

'She thinks we're new money,' Mum said when she'd sent Babs off to fetch what might have been the twentieth wedding dress, 'and not good enough for her.'

It gave me an odd feeling seeing Lal in a wedding dress. It was as if I suddenly saw not just how beautiful my big sister was, but how – well, precious. And how I really did want her to be happy, and didn't want anything awful or evil to happen to her, but maybe most of all how I didn't want her to go away. I got quite a lump in my throat thinking about it. All the times she bossed me about, or told me I was an idiot, or, in the garden, stung my legs with nettles when she wanted me to go away, or sent me to bed early because some boyfriend or other was coming round – all those times sort of faded away and I just remembered that it was always Lal I went to when I was in trouble at school, Lal who talked Mum and Dad into letting me stay up late or wear nylons instead of socks, Lal who cut my hair when Mum wanted me to keep my plaits, Lal who was ready to sit on the end of my bed and natter until midnight and then raid the fridge. What would life be like without her around every single day?

The three of us took the train out of town. Mum was all jubilant because we'd bought not only Lal's wedding dress but my bridesmaid's dress, and because she'd sat on one of those little gilt chairs and flourished her cheque book under snooty Babs's nose. Lal looked as if she was completely exhausted by love and happiness. She shut her eyes and kept them closed for the whole journey but there was a small smile on her face, as if she was imagining her wedding day, as if other than making me her bridesmaid, she was ready to abandon me without a second thought. I felt miserable and angry and then I felt guilty for feeling miserable and angry.

The bridesmaid's dress – pink satin with a layer of net over it and a scattering of little bows – was in a tissue-papered box at my feet. There was a rosebud headband to go with it and a pair of pink ballet shoes. When I'd looked at myself in the long mirror of Cripps with the snooty Babs standing behind me smiling a bright red meaningless smile, it was almost as if it wasn't me in the mirror. The girl staring back at me looked as if she'd never had a nasty thought or feeling in her life.

'Doesn't she look sweet?' Babs had cooed and I could tell Mum thought so too. She was wearing what Lal calls her 'clucky mother hen' look which she gets when she happens to feel proud of us. Rarely, in my case.

'Pretty,' Mum said firmly. As if pretty was OK and Babs's 'sweet' wasn't.

'Who'd have thought!' Lal had said. 'My sweet and pretty little sister!'

I'd given her my very best scowl but she'd only laughed.

Actually, it wasn't only that the girl in the mirror really *did* look sweet and pretty and, as I'd grumbled, 'about eleven'; what had given me a sudden shiver was the notion that there were two of me. A kind of *home* me and an *away* me, like they say at football matches. The little sister me who was good and mostly kind, the girl Alice and Dottie knew, and then this other me, the one lurking inside me, eager for danger and risk, for something that could be as wild as the sea was in winter. For Natalie.

Perhaps it was that shiver in front of the mirror or all the poshness of Cripps and the unbearable Babs – that and feeling miserable about the wedding – which made me decide, almost as soon as we got home, that I'd go and find Natalie. So what if she'd never asked me round to her house? I'd just turn up. If Natalie tested me, I could test her, couldn't I?

Mum had taken off her town dress and put a pinny on top of her old faded dress. Lal had gone off to her bedroom clutching the pad of airmail paper.

'Town's tiring,' Mum said. 'We'll all feel better when we've had something to eat.'

'I don't want anything,' I said. 'I'm going to see Natalie.'

'Natalie, Natalie,' Mum chanted. 'Who is this Natalie and why do you never bring her home?'

'Just because . . .' I said.

'No going off the beaten track,' Mum said, as she always did. 'And back by seven. Understood?'

'Understood!' I shouted, banging the front door behind me. I'd carefully not mentioned going to Natalie's house because Mum would immediately want to know where she lived. It was lucky she hadn't got round to asking me where I was meeting Natalie.

I probably wouldn't have known Natalie's exact address if it hadn't been written on the old bag that Philip took to school. I imagined Natalie had written it on the flap in case he should get lost or maybe had one of his funny turns when he didn't know where he was. I'd taken to thinking of the incident at the swimming pool as Philip's funny turn. I'd heard Mum talking about someone 'having a funny turn', and it seemed to mean someone doing something that was a bit daft or behaving in an odd way. 'A funny turn' sounded a lot less alarming than someone having the gift of second sight.

To get to Natalie's I had to go along the beach road to the far end before taking the road that ran down to the station. It was late afternoon. Everyone had probably gone off for their tea because there was hardly anyone on the beach apart from the artist. I could just see him way off by the slipway. It looked as if he'd made a campfire and was cooking something. I wondered what he did all winter. Mum said he must do something to earn some money because he couldn't earn much from his paintings.

'Some paintings are worth thousands,' I'd said. 'Our art teacher told us.'

Mum laughed. 'Those are paintings by dead artists. People like Van Gogh or Matisse. Paintings in galleries.'

'Well, maybe our artist will be one of them when he's dead,' I said. (*Our artist*, that's how I thought of him at the beginning of the summer and long before I thought of him as *my artist*.)

Mum had only laughed again and said she thought it was unlikely.

The walk to Natalie's took me from the rich to the poor end of Norton. There were the elegant houses overlooking the sea, several storeys tall, some of them with small balconies. Turning off the sea road took you down long streets of squat terraces all huddled together. Unlike the tall houses, which looked as if the people who lived in them lived grandly happy lives, the terraced houses had an anxious look as if the people who lived in them lived scared and worried lives, working hard and doing what they were told.

Beyond these streets was the council estate. It looked as if the houses had been thrown together in a higgledy-piggledy way and no one much cared about them, neither the council nor the people who lived there. No one had bothered to paint the front doors or windows. Most of the gardens were just weedy patches with broken fences or gates.

I'd never been here before. It was one of Mum's off-the-beaten-track places. It was hard to work out the streets on the estate. They took off, one from another, like a creature continually growing new legs. They seemed to be named after saints, as if to encourage people to be saintly. I didn't know there were quite so many saints. I wandered around St Patrick's, St Brigid's, St Peter's and St Stephen's until I found Natalie's.

There were kids playing out in the street, two women having a loud argument, a man in braces pumping up the tyres of his bike and, from Natalie's house – 42 St Andrew's Street – the sound of her mother shrieking at someone and Natalie joining in. It was scary and exciting and a world away from the silent, lace-curtained respectability of my street where even Mum's laugh seemed too loud.

The person being shrieked at was a man. He came out of the house dragging on his jacket, his face bruised. Natalie's mother, dressed in a faded kimono, had a poker in her hand and seemed about to follow him down the path, only Natalie held her back.

'He's not worth it!' Natalie shouted at his back.

The man hunched the collar of his jacket up, scowled at her and slunk away. I hesitated on the corner by the broken fence. I was suddenly aware that I was still in my best going-to-town clothes – a summer dress that tied in a bow at the back, and the new sandals Mum had polished that morning.

Natalie didn't look pleased to see me. 'You'd better come in,' she said.

'Who's this?' asked her mother. I could see she was a once-beautiful woman. I thought maybe she was like the woman in Lal's *True Romances* who'd been 'ravaged by love'. She had the same wild dark hair as Natalie, the same intense brown eyes, though she'd added purple eye shadow and thick black mascara. The skin of her face – the exact oval of Natalie's – was pulled so tight that she was all sharp cheekbones with hollows underneath. I couldn't be certain, but I thought she had nothing on under the faded but exotic kimono that was just about the exact opposite of Mum's warm and woolly dressing gown.

'This is Lizzie,' said Natalie.

'How d'you do, Lizzie,' said her mother. 'Welcome to our humble abode.'

I could tell she was being sarcastic by the tone of her voice and the way she looked me up and down as if working out just what sort of family I came from and how much money we had.

'Thank you, Mrs Rafferty,' I said, and blushed.

'Oh, don't mention it!' she said, in the same sarcastic tone. 'We're not hoity toity here, are we, Nat?'

'Ignore her,' Natalie said. 'I'm about to get the tea.'

'Maybe I shouldn't have come,' I said. I was so embarrassed I felt all clumsy and awkward.

'You're staying,' she told me.

I followed her into the front room, a sitting room of sorts. I'd been about to ask where Philip was when Natalie said, 'You can come out now, Phil,' and a tear-stained face appeared from behind the sofa.

'Get him out of here,' Mrs Rafferty said, sitting herself in front of an enormous television and putting her feet up on an old chair.

I wondered if she ever got dressed. It seemed rather fine never to bother. Perhaps if you were ravaged by love you didn't. Next to what to eat – or maybe before – what to wear was Mum's main interest in life.

Philip didn't need telling. He trailed after us into the kitchen. Still with her eyes fixed on the television, Mrs Rafferty slapped the backs of his legs as he went past her.

The kitchen faced the railway line. Whenever a train went by – and two did – the whole room shook and you couldn't hear yourself speak. The kitchen walls were half pale grey and half dark green and splotched with old grease. There was a big fridge in the corner which every now and again shook itself alive, gave a massive rattle then fell silent again.

I was keen to help but it was hard to know what to do. The sink was full of dirty dishes. I couldn't help noticing half a bottle of gin standing on the window ledge along with a row of empty beer bottles. There wasn't what you could call a proper table like we had at home. I think it was a fold-up card table with a newspaper as a cloth. There were two chairs and a stool with telephone directories on top so that anyone sitting on it could reach the table. Squashed into the corner was a lopsided sofa, the springs coming out of the bottom of it, one arm lost altogether. Philip hunched himself up on it. From somewhere inside it he pulled out a colourless old blanket. He sniffed and sucked at one end of it, watching us – or maybe just me – wary as a cat.

'Wipe your nose,' Natalie ordered. (Philip used the other corner of the blanket.) 'And give me your specs.'

Philip handed them over. Natalie cleaned the thick lenses with the edge of her skirt. One arm of the specs was bound up with sellotape. For a moment I had the mad notion that Natalie was rubbing some kind of magic into the specs, that it was she who gave him what she called 'the gift'. I think it was the strangeness of the afternoon that did it, going from the posh city store to 42 St Andrew's Street, from Lal's wedding dress to Philip's smelly bit of blanket. The two halves of my life coming a bit too close together. I hoped Philip wasn't going to do any Seeing just then. I didn't think I could cope.

'You can have beans on toast or beans on toast,' Natalie told him. 'What would you like?'

That made Philip giggle. He put his specs back on and gave Natalie a wobbly smile. 'I'll have b-b-beans on t-t-toast!' he said.

From the next room Mrs Rafferty shouted, 'How long do I have to bloody wait? And I'll have mine with a cuppa. Did you get more sugar?'

Natalie emptied two cans of beans into a pan, shoved bread under the grill, switched on the kettle and put a spoonful of tea in a strainer over a mug. 'When it's bloody ready,' she shouted back. 'And I borrowed the sugar. Again.'

Philip stayed on the sofa for his tea. Natalie gave him the pan and a spoon. She cut the toast into chunks and put it in with the beans for him. Mrs Rafferty had her tea on a tray. With a cuppa. Natalie and I sat at the card table.

I thought of tea back home. The white cloth with the fringed damask one underneath. Mum serving Dad. What might it be? Ham and chips, maybe, and then a pie with cream. And there'd be the usual conversation about how tough it was during the war when food was rationed and you couldn't get eggs and you couldn't get cream. Then as soon as we'd finished, everything would be washed up and put away and it was television time. I thought Mum would be quite shocked if she could see me here eating beans on toast on a table covered in newspapers. Whatever else you could say about Natalie's house, you couldn't call it 'nice'. I was glad. I was as bored with niceness as I was with peace.

'I suppose you have a big tea with cake and things,' Natalie said. She'd finished her beans before me. Now she sat with her elbows on the table, chin in her hands, watching me. I couldn't tell if she was pleased to see me or not.

'Well, sometimes,' I said. 'Sometimes we have cake.'

'And wine?' said Natalie. 'Do your parents drink wine?'

'No,' I said. 'They like lemonade. Pop, Mum calls it.'

'Pop!' Natalie echoed. 'And does your dad make lots of money?'

I hesitated. I didn't exactly know. 'Well, not lots,' I said. Then, trying to change the subject, I asked her about the man I'd seen leaving. 'Who was he?' I asked. 'Your mum seemed really angry.'

It was the wrong thing to ask. Natalie cleared our bowls and dumped them in the sink without looking at me.

'Just an uncle,' she said, all sharp and shut off from me.

'L-l-lots of b-b-bastard uncles,' Philip said from the depths of the sofa.

'Shut up!' Natalie said, throwing an old magazine at his head. 'We're a big family,' she told me. 'Philip muddles people up.'

I wanted to ask about the missing dad but it didn't feel like the right moment.

'Lucky you,' I said, 'having a big family.' I was thinking of the uncles, aunts and cousins once, twice and for ever removed because of Mum marrying out.

I was still hungry after the beans but there obviously wasn't anything else to eat and I told myself that this was a natural hunger, not the sort I get at home, which was – how could I describe it? – a kind of hunger of the heart.

'I suppose I'd better go,' I said.

'No,' said Natalie. 'Not yet.' She tiptoed over to the door and looked in at her mother. Mrs Rafferty was fast asleep. Natalie shut the door very quietly. Even with the door closed she still whispered.

'It's time I told you the plan,' she said.

Natalie's Diary

Monday

Lizzie's in! I've told her. As soon as the holidays start we can begin.

Didn't tell her like I meant to tell her. The Plan. Was going to tell it all calm and clear. Came out when I couldn't hold it in any longer. It was Ma of course. Ma always wrecks everything.

Then Lizzie just turning up like that. Out the blue, like Ma says of Dodgy Doug, though I don't know what she means by that. Dodgy Doug (Philip calls him that) turns up whenever. Not out the blue. Out the black and blue, if you ask me. Not that anyone does.

Well, Lizzie just turned up and you shouldn't do that. Turn up on someone, like, without warning, even if you are kindred spirits. Which we are. My idea, of course.

Saturday afternoon. Tea time. Worst possible time. Ma out in the street with a poker in her hand chasing Dodgy Doug away. Lizzie arriving all neat and pretty in a summer dress. Eyes popping out her head when she sees Ma. Ma in her kimono with not much on underneath, waving the poker like it was a copper's truncheon.

Ma shouting so everyone can hear. *Think this is a free service, do you? Don't come back without your wallet!*

Pavement, swallow me up, I'm thinking.

Why can't Ma dress proper?

Why can't I have a proper ma?

NB to Self. Find proper ma. Ha ha ha.

Philip hiding like he always does. *Little Freak,* Ma calls him. *Freak. Freak. Freak.*

Philip thinks *Freak* means *Special.* That's what I tell him. Suppose he'll find out what it really means one day.

Ma with poker. Philip hiding behind sofa. Lizzie not knowing what to do. On one leg. On the other leg. Red in the face in her fancy frock with a bow at the back. Doesn't know what to do with herself, twisting her hands together like that.

I nearly say, *Go. Go away and don't come back till I ask you!* Then something goes *ping* in my head and I think, *Now! Now's the time! The time is right.* Maybe that's what they call instinct.

NB to Self. Maybe Philip's got the Gift but I've got Instinct. Work on it.

Philip's bugging me. He's been dreaming of Da again. At least he says it's Da. How can he know? He can't remember Da like I do, even though I was only six. Philip says he 'Sees' Da in some place where there's a fence made of wire and Da can't get out. And that's just how it was in Colditz, though Philip can't know that. Sometimes when he's awake and Seeing, I don't know what he's talking about. Does he know the difference between yesterday and tomorrow? Last year and next year? Goodness knows.

Lately he's taken to saying, 'Not going to grow up. Not never.' Really scary! So I turn it into a joke. 'Of course you're going to grow up, Phil, everyone grows up,' I say and I tickle him until he says he will too.

Where was I? Ma's out in the street and Lizzie's standing there with her mouth open. So I just yank her in. Ma goes all smarmy and sarcastic then and Lizzie goes all pink and polite like she's been told to do.

NB to Self. Being polite can almost strangle a person so they can't say what they really think.

At last – when I'm ready to tear my hair out – Ma shuts herself in with the telly and there's Lizzie, Philip and me in the kitchen. The relief! I make us all beans on toast. Stretching it. All the time I'm rehearsing in my head how I'm going to tell her. The words I'll use. Lizzie's all eyes, taking everything in as if she's on holiday in a foreign country. I don't care that she doesn't invite me to her posh house. I don't think I'd know how to be all fake and polite. Anyway, the way she looked around the kitchen here, anyone would think she thought coming to a council estate and eating baked beans on toast was an adventure! An adventure! She can't know what a serious adventure this is going to be.

I wish she hadn't asked about Dodgy Doug. I had to lie. Pretend he was an uncle. Then Philip nearly gave the game away, talking about lots of bastard uncles. I think Philip hates the men more than I do. Sometimes one of them will ask him his name. Philip never answers. When they ask Ma, she just says, 'Oh, he's my mistake.'

Mistake or a freak, that's what she calls Philip. When I'm grown up, I'm going to take Philip away with me. Me, Lizzie and Philip. When the danger's over we could live somewhere where there's real peace, not this pretend stuff. Philip likes Lizzie. The Plan wouldn't work if he didn't. She saved him from drowning – he's not going to forget that.

When we'd had tea, I waited until Ma had fallen asleep. You can never tell with Ma if she'll suddenly barge in on you. I wanted somewhere safe. Somewhere with a bolt on the door. I took Lizzie up to my room. Philip didn't need telling. He was right behind us.

Once I'd bolted the door, I thought I had what I wanted to say all prepared. But I couldn't hold it in any longer. Lizzie's standing there, all expectant. Waiting. And it just burst out of me.

'The thing is, Lizzie,' I said, 'there are Left-Over Nazis.'

Lizzie just gaped at me. 'Where?' she asked. 'Where?'

'Everywhere,' I said.

Chapter 5

Because How Can Evil Stop?

As soon as we were in Natalie's bedroom she bolted the door and put a chair under the handle.

When my eyes got used to the dark – there was only one window and it was covered by a poster – I thought I'd walked into something out of *The Arabian Nights*. Natalie switched on a small lamp. There was hardly anything in the way of furniture apart from a tin box, a mirror with most of its silver backing worn away so you could only see part of yourself in it, and two mattresses on the floor, each one covered in a mix of old coats, shawls and tattered tartan rugs. Obviously Natalie shared the room with Philip.

She must have been to umpteen jumble sales to collect the cloths that were pinned across the walls in great swags or tied up with ribbons or string. You couldn't see the walls for drapes of silk and velvet and cottons in all sorts of colours and patterns. The room couldn't have been more different from the bleak and greasy kitchen downstairs. Natalie had made this room into a kind of magical tent, a room of many colours. I thought the room was as magical and exotic as Natalie was and I loved it.

Philip had taken to one of the mattresses, wrapping himself into a tartan rug. Squatting there, he looked like the little dumpling Buddha I'd seen in the junk shop window.

When Natalie switched on the lamp I could see that the poster over the window was the old wartime one I'd seen in a magazine. It was a faded picture of a man called Kitchener pointing his finger at us. The slogan underneath read YOUR COUNTRY NEEDS YOU.

'What have you got that up there for?' I asked, because it didn't seem to match the rest of the room.

And that's when she told me. About the Left-Over Nazis. About The Plan.

'Sleepers,' she called them at first, as if she was letting me into her world, her crazy quest.

'All over the country,' Natalie said. 'Sleepers. Waiting. Waiting in villages like ours for orders.'

'Sleepers?' I sat down on the other mattress. Natalie was pacing the room.

'Left-Over Nazis,' she said. 'Waiting until we're all half asleep. Then they'll rise again . . .'

'Because how can evil just stop . . . ?' I said. It had come back to me, what she'd said that day at The Baths when Philip had had his funny turn. If it *was* a funny turn.

Natalie was really excited now. 'Yes! Yes!' she said. 'Evil's like – well, it's like the plague. It doesn't just go away. It lies waiting, sleeping, ready to come back again.'

I thought of the plague – the Black Death we'd learned about in history. I thought about how people say that one bad apple can make all the others bad. I thought of how Mum was always telling me not to get in with what she called 'a bad crowd'. Somehow it all seemed connected. And Natalie had to be right. Of course evil couldn't stop! Bad people didn't become good people overnight. Had there ever been a time in the whole history of the world when there hadn't been evil? But was she right about the Left-Over Nazis?

Natalie crouched down beside me. 'They've never found Hitler's body, you know,' she said. 'What d'you think a whole defeated country would want?'

Philip jumped up as if he'd been waiting for this bit. 'Revenge! Revenge! Revenge!' he chanted.

Natalie hushed him. 'To put us all in concentration camps,' she said. 'Starting with the Jews, of course. Your mother's Jewish, isn't she?'

She slipped the question in so slyly that a shudder went right through me. It was as though all the stories about the war had been lodged inside me, locked up somewhere just under my heart, as if in a box, and now Natalie had opened it and dragged up a dread like an awful sickness. Maybe if you were a baby during the war, war got into your head – the bombs, the fear, the fighting, the dying – without you knowing and you could never, ever get rid of it. I didn't ask Natalie how she knew about my mum. Maybe she'd seen her in the street. Maybe it was Mum's nose – her *snozzle*, as Dad calls it – or her loud laugh. Whatever it is about her that tells people she's Jewish.

'If she's Jewish, so are you,' Natalie continued. 'It follows the mother's line, you know. You could have died in a concentration camp.'

She said it as casually as if I'd just missed being run over by a bus.

'Starving! Starving! Starving!' chanted Philip.

'Well, I didn't,' I said, almost apologetically.

It's funny the things you know without quite knowing that you know them. So although I'd known that Mum being Jewish meant that Lal and I were too, I hadn't really let it into the knowing part of my mind. We were cut off, was all I'd thought. Cut off from faith and family.

'My dad did,' Natalie said calmly. 'A prisoner-of-war camp. Colditz.'

'I'm sorry,' I said lamely. 'Sorry.'

My own dad, who when I was little I thought had won the war all by himself, suddenly seemed less heroic for *not* dying.

'How d'you know? How d'you know about the – the Sleepers?' I asked desperately. 'About them waiting?'

'My dad told me.'

'Your dad? But he's . . .'

'Dead. I know. But he speaks to Philip. Philip can See him. He speaks to Philip. Then Philip tells me.'

'How? When?'

I wanted this to be all wrong. Made up. Crazy.

Natalie sighed as if this was unnecessary, as if I shouldn't want proof. 'Some nights,' she said, 'Philip wakes me up and tells me. I write it down.'

She knelt in front of the tin box and eased off the lid. 'Background research,' she said. I thought of the invisible box hidden under my heart, the box of dreads. Peering over Natalie's shoulder, I got a glimpse of what looked like stolen library books. I could see library numbers and letters on the spines. There were folded newspaper cuttings too. Photos of Hitler or SS men, the cover of a magazine showing concentration camp victims, skeletons, almost, in their striped pyjama outfits. It made me shiver just to look at them. Natalie pulled out a small black notebook. It said MESSAGES on the cover. She flipped through it until she found the page she wanted, then pushed it over to me.

'Read!' she said.

I read. Philip put his fingers in his ears.

'He doesn't like hearing them again,' Natalie said.

Still in hiding was the first message. After that, dated, came *The swastika flies high* and *Find them out! SS in hiding*. The last one Natalie had written down was *False peace! False peace!*

Natalie took the book from me and put it back in the tin box. 'Well?' she said. 'Well?'

And I knew she was waiting for me to say, 'Yes, yes, I believe it all.' And I knew that if I didn't, it would be the end of kindred spirits.

I looked at Philip squatting on the mattress and giving me his wobbly smile. Could he communicate with the dead? Talk to his dead father? Get messages? And why would the father choose Philip and not Natalie? The answer to that one seemed obvious. Philip was innocent, open. Maybe we all started off life with the Gift, able to See, but then it left us as we grew older. Without knowing it, there were senses we shut off.

Natalie waited. Unbolted the door. Was she about to send me away?

'You can join us, Lizzie,' she said. 'If you want, that is. Join us in tracking them down. The Sleepers. The Left-Over Nazis.'

'Yes!' I said. 'Yes!'

The Caravan
Midnight

Dear Helena,
I'm sorry. I know I promised to write every week but somehow time here by the sea doesn't seem to go in weeks. That's a poor excuse, I know. Anyway, you'll be pleased to hear that I've been working hard. Not much painting yet but lots of sketches, and I'm excited about them.

Remember the children I told you about? It's school holidays now so they're on the beach a lot. Of course there are other people about – the usual folk, mums and toddlers, old men with dogs, hikers in walking boots, etc. etc. – and I do rough sketches of them, but mainly for practice. My three – that's how I think of them, my three – are the ones that interest me.

The two girls are obviously best friends. The Wild One and the Dreamy One, I call them, because I don't know their names yet. Either they're walking with their arms about each other as if they're Siamese twins or they're sitting in a kind of huddle, their heads together like a couple of witches, talking really seriously. About what? I hear you ask. I've no idea. Whatever it is looks important. And urgent. I'd really like to get all three of them to pose for me so I could do portraits of them, but I don't want to rush them or scare them off. Best to get to know them slowly, I think. When they do notice me, the Wild One looks at me as if I'm a crab that's just crawled out of the sea. The Dreamy One smiles, but only when the Wild One's not looking!

At the moment it's the boy who interests me most. And I know his name, because he's told me. It's Philip. Quite often the girls forget about him and he wanders up the beach to me. I think the caravan appeals to him. He's an odd little soul. Tufty hair, a bit of a limp, specs. Looks neglected. Seems to wear the same jersey – with holes – for weeks at a time. At first he just stood looking at the caravan. Wouldn't come too close, like a shy kitten. Wouldn't take a biscuit when I offered one. So I just carried on sitting on the stool with the easel in front of me, working on a picture or two of the fishing boats. Curiosity made him come nearer and nearer. So when he got close enough I said, 'My name's Hugo. What's yours?'

He's got a bit of a stutter, but eventually he got it out. 'Ph-Ph-Philip.'

Now that we've exchanged names, he's more relaxed. But this is the really strange thing about him. He seems to know things. I mean, things he can't really know. The other day he was just sitting on an old fish box, watching me, when he says, 'B-b-brother!' And points a finger at me.

'A sister,' I said. 'And you've got a sister too. She calls you and you go running.'

That made him giggle. But then he shook his head and said, 'No . . . you've got a b-b-brother.'

'I've a sister,' I said. 'Her name's Helena.'

At which he nodded very gravely as if he knew this all along and said, 'B-b-but I seen boy.'

Perhaps my paintings have confused him. And I know, I know. It's best not to start thinking back. I hardly ever get those flashbacks these days. When I was with Aunt Em I was forever seeing them: the Gestapo storming the stairs. Mum screaming. Uncle Reuben dragging us away. It being too late for Jo. I must paint it out, paint it out. That's the only way. And I know that's what you keep telling me to do.

Well, I mustn't start imagining all sorts. Let's be reasonable. As far as Philip's concerned, the most likely explanation is that while I was in the caravan making a cup of tea, he looked through my sketchpad and saw a picture of you. You when you were looking rather boyish, wearing shorts and with your hair cropped. And that gave him the idea of a brother.

Though that doesn't quite explain why he then said, 'R-r-red hair. Like you. Like fire.'

The sketches are in charcoal. Well, I suppose he was just guessing.

I'll send you a picture of him when I can. And I promise to write again soon.

Tell Derek I'll aim to have some new paintings for the gallery by the autumn.

Lots of love,
Hugo

Chapter 6

The Vow

'The air-raid shelter,' Natalie said. 'It can be our place. Meet me there at three.'

I was more scared of the air-raid shelter than I'd been of the pier. The shelter was one of the few sights left in Norton that told you there'd been a war. We had one bomb site – just a kind of bleak field where even a scrubby kind of grass found it a struggle to grow – a few prefabs (cheap tin bungalows which Mum said were used as temporary houses when the real ones had been bombed), and the air-raid shelter.

It had been put up on the sand hills. When I was little, I thought the sand hills were like a desert. Actually they were just made of sand blown in from the sea for years and years and years and years until they turned into hills or dunes. And that's where they'd put the air-raid shelter. Our geography teacher said that once upon a time there was a forest under our village but the sand had covered it over. Sometimes the shelter looked as if it was sinking under the sand like the forest had done. Other times – when it was dusk or the sky went dark before rain – it looked as if it was the sand that was sinking and the shelter rising up. Rising up like Natalie said the Left-Over Nazis were going to do.

I liked the idea of a den, only not the dark air-raid shelter with its big door that was wedged open with sand but which I felt could shut you in for ever. Also I'd loved the first week of the school holidays when we'd just messed about on the beach or talked about what we were going to be when we'd left school and were grown up enough to leave home.

Natalie was going to be a journalist – a foreign correspondent, she said. 'You know, the one who is sent wherever there's danger. Philip and I will have a flat – no, an apartment – in New York. You can visit, Lizzie.'

I think she only added that, about me visiting, when she saw me looking sulky. I hated being excluded from anything Natalie had in mind. *Kindred spirits*, she'd said and kept on saying, and to me that meant for ever and wherever. Was it the same for her? I didn't think so. How could anyone pin that wildness of hers down? Or even want to. Natalie could never quite belong to the ordinary, everyday world. At least, that's how I felt about her. And I had to try not to mind and just count myself lucky to have her in my life in whatever way she chose.

Messing about on the beach wasn't enough for Natalie. She was restless and moody. Whenever she could she'd turn the conversation to LONs. That's what we called them now, the Left-Over Nazis. LONs. It made them sound like a pop group or something. It was like our secret code. No one else would know what we were talking about.

'We've got to begin,' Natalie kept saying. 'Got to begin tracking them down.'

'Whenever you say,' I said. I didn't have a clue what she really had in mind.

'When Philip's ready,' she said.

'We're waiting for Philip?'

'I've told you,' Natalie said irritably. 'Philip can see. When he sees them, he'll know them. The LONs.' She pulled me close to her. In almost a whisper she added, 'He can see inside people.'

I didn't know what to make of it – of Philip seeing inside people as if he had X-ray eyes. And it was soon after Natalie had told me this that she came up with the idea of the air-raid shelter as our place. Or our HQ, as she called it later.

'Imagine,' she said, on our first meeting there, 'the air-raid warning going off in the middle of the night!' She whooped an imitation of the siren, holding her nose and throwing her head back. Philip put his hands over his ears. 'And everyone huddling in here listening to the bombs. Did your ma come here? Has she told you?'

'No,' I said. 'We've got a passage that goes down to the garage. That's where we hid. We've still got a gas mask.'

'A gas mask! They've kept it!' Natalie looked as excited as if I'd told her we had a ghost in the cellar. 'Will you bring it? Bring it here?'

'If you want,' I said. I was pleased there was something I could give her (apart from undying friendship, that is), even if it was something as strange as a gas mask. It hung – horribly like a pig's head with a long snout – in our unused larder. I wasn't sure how to smuggle it out of the house but I didn't think anyone would miss it.

Within the shelter Natalie had used an old coal shovel to make a kind of seat of sand for herself. She'd found a piece of seaweed and wound it round her head. She looked wonderful sitting there with a seaweed crown, letting Philip sprinkle her bare toes with sand.

'We can make this our place,' she said. 'Yours and mine. Kindred spirits, eh?'

'We could bring things,' I said vaguely. 'Make it more homely.'

Natalie frowned. 'Just bring the gas mask,' she said.

So I did. I shoved it into an old shopping bag like a decapitated head with a towel stuffed round it. It was a pity Lal saw me taking it. She peered into the bag and went, 'Yuck! What d'you want that for?' She was off to post yet another letter to Paul and didn't wait for an answer. 'Where did they get you from?' she asked on her way out, the way she always did.

'Mars,' I shouted back, like I always did. She must have forgotten about it because she didn't ask any more questions. I don't think there was any space in Lal's head for questions – unless they were questions to do with Paul or the wedding.

Natalie crowed over the gas mask, dragging it over her head, grunting and making the snout waggle until Philip screamed, 'Piggy! Piggy! Piggy!' half in fright, half in delight, before he burst into tears and Natalie took it off.

'Can I keep it?'

'What d'you want it for?'

She gave me a long considering look as if there were some questions I shouldn't need to ask. 'We might need it,' was all she would say.

After that the gas mask was hidden under an old fish box, and Natalie's *Messages* notebook, which she'd kept in the tin box in her bedroom, now lived under two stones. It was all part of making the shelter 'our place'.

'Before it's really and truly our place – our HQ' – this was the first time Natalie had called the shelter that – 'we have to make a Vow.'

She had it prepared on some stiff art paper I recognized as coming from school, which she'd made into a scroll. The Vow said:

I, Natalie Rafferty, and I, Lizzie Worthing, hereby vow undying friendship, and that we, together with Philip Rafferty, hereby pledge to rout out evil from the world, and in particular to find and expose all members of the Gestapo still lurking undercover and waiting to dominate the world, putting all Jews and their kin to death.

Philip couldn't read properly yet so we let him decorate the Vow. He drew a skull and crossbones in red and black wax crayons. Tongue between his teeth, he added a big careful P for Philip. Then Natalie and I signed our names, and Natalie rolled up the scroll, slid it into a biscuit tin and made a hole to hide it in.

For the rest of that week we met in the shelter every afternoon. At each meeting Natalie took the scroll out of the biscuit tin and we read it out loud. Philip soon had it by heart. Some afternoons Natalie brought along books she'd stolen from the library. I knew she'd stolen them because I could see where she'd torn out the slip in the front with the borrowing dates stamped on it saying when the book should be returned. She read out passages to Philip and me. It was part of what she called *your preparation*.

One of the books was *The Diary of Anne Frank*, which I'd already read. Somehow it sounded different when Natalie read out the bit about older people not wavering in their opinions and acts whereas it was much harder for young people – here Natalie gave me a fierce look – to hold their ground and stick to their opinions.

'Don't waver,' Philip repeated. 'M-m-maintain our 'pinions.'

It was summer, it was July, it was sunny, but those dark afternoons in the shelter with Anne Frank's *Diary* meant I could hardly stop thinking about concentration camps and how it might be possible to survive all manner of terrible physical ordeals, but if your spirit was broken, that was it. I thought my own spirit might be pretty flimsy, unlike Natalie's. Natalie, I thought, would never waver. As she sat cross-legged in the shelter, the seaweed crown on her head, looking fiercely at Philip and me, I thought Natalie's spirit was like a small clear flame of fiery, angry conviction.

Apart from *The Diary of Anne Frank*, the library book that really pleased her was all about some Nazi prisoners of war. 'There was a plot,' Natalie read aloud, 'in December 1944, hatched by some Nazi prisoners of war in camp twenty-three, near Devizes in Wiltshire, which held seven thousand men, to stage a mass escape. They planned to kill the guards, seize their weapons and free POWs from other camps. They would then make an assault on London.'

'If those prisoners of war had really escaped from Devizes and collected lots of other prisoners, they'd have attacked London by now,' I said.

Natalie frowned. 'Have you never hated anyone?' she asked.

Somehow the way she asked the question made me feel I was a failure if I hadn't hated anyone, as if it was a lack of passion, as if I was hardly fit to be a kindred spirit without an anger that matched Natalie's.

'There's people I don't like . . .' I offered.

'Not the same,' she said.

'I don't see what this has got to do with the prisoners of war in Devizes,' I said, trying to defend myself. (Actually, back at home I'd looked up Wiltshire and Devizes in the atlas and had been relieved to see that it was quite a long way from Norton.)

'There were seven thousand prisoners in camp twenty-three,' said Natalie. 'And maybe their escape plan didn't work out. In the book it says the records have been lost so no one really knows the exact number. Maybe only *some* of them escaped. Maybe there weren't enough to allow them to go round releasing other prisoners and form a new army to attack London. But maybe the few that *did* escape found others, went into hiding here in England, waited for more to come – to come secretly from Germany. If you hated someone, really hated them so that you wanted revenge, you'd wait. Five, ten, fifteen years. However long it took.'

All those numbers swam about in my head. I wanted to know about hate. I wanted to know about love. Did both last and last and last? You'd want love to last, but hate?

'Who d'you hate?' I asked Natalie.

She gave me a withering look. 'I thought that would have been obvious by now,' she said. 'The SS. The Nazis who let my dad die. The ones who are still alive when he isn't.'

I'd become almost jealous of Natalie's dead father. I felt bad about it. I remembered how I'd felt jealous of Alice when she had a baby sister, but it's one thing to be jealous of a baby sister. Natural. Not bad. I knew I should feel things like sorrow and sympathy about Natalie's dead father, not envy. What was the matter with me that I seemed to be spending the summer not feeling what I thought I *ought* to feel? Like I should be feeling sorry for Natalie and happy for Lal, and I didn't feel either. I tried to bend my feelings in the way they should go, as if feelings were like paper clips and you could straighten them out.

Part of feeling jealous of Natalie's dad was that I knew my

own dad hadn't been in the army or navy or air force during the war. He'd been exempt because he was in one of the trades the government said was essential. He'd been given fire-watching duties instead, though if he'd ever had to fight a fire no one had mentioned it. What with Mum marrying out and being cut off, and Dad being exempt, I seemed to come from a family that refused to be part of anything.

And then I couldn't help thinking that if it wasn't for Natalie's dad, we wouldn't be sitting here in the damp shelter on a summer's afternoon. We'd started *Hamlet* at school. We'd done the opening scene when the ghost of Hamlet's father appears. Natalie's dad wasn't exactly a ghost, but he was the next best thing – 'communicating', as Natalie called it, with Philip, firing up his daughter.

There was no way that Natalie was going to let go of the prisoner-of-war story. 'You've got to understand that it could take years,' she said. 'It could take until now to gather a secret army. They'd have Sleepers hidden. Spies and saboteurs. Left-Over Nazis hiding all over the country. Especially in places no one would think of looking.'

'Like Norton,' I said.

'Exactly!' said Natalie. I saw that she'd pulled a shawl out of her satchel. It was black and silky and embroidered with what looked like peacocks and flowers. It reminded me of her mother's kimono. Perhaps she'd 'borrowed' it. Wherever it had come from, she draped it around her shoulders so that its long fringe hung down to her waist while she strutted about the shelter. Philip and I gazed up at her. I thought she looked like a gypsy queen who could enchant anyone.

Norton, the village where I'd grown up, where the most exciting thing that I could remember ever happening was the lifeboat going out to rescue three fishermen one stormy winter night, was suddenly peopled in my imagination with the spies and saboteurs, the escaped prisoners of war, Natalie's Left-Over Nazis.

'What do we have to do?' I asked, hoping the fear that seemed to be turning my stomach inside out didn't show.

It was obviously the right question. Showed Natalie's *preparation* was working. She knelt down in front of me and took my hands.

'There's information,' she said. 'Philip's had another dream!'

'A dream?' Could a dream and information be one and the same thing?

Philip himself had found an old stick in the corner of the shelter and was drawing patterns in the sand.

'Philip's dreams are more like visions,' Natalie said, as if she'd heard the doubt in my voice. 'I've told you. He gets messages from our father.'

For a ridiculous moment I thought she meant Our Father Who Art in Heaven, and then I remembered the messages she'd written down in her black *Messages* book about the SS in hiding and the *False Peace, False Peace*. The messages had been – still were – scary, but somehow scary like a bad horoscope that warns you of something awful without telling you what.

'OK,' I said carefully. 'So what's the message? Does it tell us what to do?' I didn't want to say, 'Does *he* tell us what to do?' I didn't want to believe in their dad as a ghost.

Natalie brought Philip away from his game with the stick. She sat him in front of her and wrapped the shawl around him.

'Tell!' she said. 'Tell Lizzie your dream.'

Philip shut his eyes and began rocking to and fro.

Behind him, Natalie shut her eyes too, as if whatever Philip was going to say had to come through her as well. If I hadn't been rooted to the spot, half terrified, half fascinated, I might have run away there and then. If it had been anyone else but Natalie I might have run . . .

'The m-man . . . with the cars . . .' Philip stuttered. 'And the g-girl with the r-ring. Very sh-shiny. How she smiles! D-Daddy says b-bad! B-bad! Find them out! Find them out!'

He stopped rocking and then began wailing. It was a queer little high-pitched wail, as though he had to learn to wail quietly.

I felt completely let down. 'Is that it?' I asked. 'Is that the information? Norton must be full of men with cars and girls with rings!'

Natalie kept Philip wrapped in the shawl until he stopped wailing. Then she fetched some paper and a black crayon from her bag and set them on the upturned fish box.

'Show her the last bit,' she instructed him. 'He can't speak it all out loud,' she said to me. 'It hurts him.'

Hunched over the paper, screwing up his eyes and sticking out his tongue, Philip outlined two swastikas and crayoned them in as if it was important not to leave any whiteness, as if he was crayoning them in and scrubbing them out all at the same time.

'Philip will know them,' Natalie said. 'The Left-Over Nazis. He'll know them when he sees them.'

'But how?' I asked, drawn back in, both believing and not wanting to believe.

In almost a whisper Natalie said, 'I've told you. He can see inside people. He can see the swastikas on their hearts!'

I stared at Philip. He was sitting up straight now and grinning proudly, looking up at Natalie to check that she was pleased with him.

'See inside!' he echoed. 'See inside!'

'That's when we start,' said Natalie. 'Start hunting them out.'

Natalie's Diary

Wednesday

Sometimes it goes right through me. Can anger burn you up? Burn up your inside so you're just walking about like an outside body but with nothing inside?

In London there were three of them just in our street and the street behind. Philip put the finger on them. He can do it here too. I keep telling him.

NB to Self. Remind Philip before he falls asleep. Show him Da's photo.

Counted three new men seeing Ma. One of them might be. We could get rid of him. They go when they think they're found out.

Money. Gin. Ma's songs.

My spitting is getting better. I can spit about three feet now. Well, from our gate almost to the end of the street. I like it. I like gathering it in my mouth. Sucking it in then spitting it out.

We've got the air-raid shelter. Philip and I could live there if we had to. If Ma went off like Da.

NB to Self. Do not be silly. Ma never sober enough to go off anywhere. Do not start thinking that way.

What if Alice and Dottie try to win Lizzie back? I think she's true. I think she's truer than anyone I know. Philip's picture of Lizzie. An anchor! Made me laugh.

Philip should keep his pictures in his head. Dangerous on paper. The swastikas are OK though. They're proof.

NB to Self. Write down Philip's dreams in the Messages book early morning.

When we've done it – routed them out – we'll be famous, Lizzie and I. Cheering crowds. They'll ask us to advise the prime minister. No, we'll say. We need a holiday!

'Make me proud of you, girl!' That's what Da said. I remember. Philip don't. What was I? Six? Philip brand new. I don't forget. Why does he choose Philip?

I think Da was good at spitting. I'm holding his hand. He spits out bits of raw tobacco from the side of his mouth. That was his smell. Tobacco.

Lizzie's smell is baby soap.

Chapter 7
In the Air-raid Shelter

Maybe it was the darkness in Natalie that both pulled me towards her yet scared me. Or maybe it was just the gloom of the air-raid shelter that made me suddenly remember the artist. His yellow caravan. The jazz I'd heard him playing. It was as if I'd almost forgotten it was summer, as if summer *was* the artist.

Natalie had gone quiet. It happened now and again. Either she and Philip were out all the time, in the street, on the beach, on the estate, or they were nowhere to be seen. 'Sometimes Ma needs me,' was all Natalie would say when I asked. I thought maybe her ma was ill or maybe all the uncles came to stay and she had to do the cooking and looking after. She was so snappy about it, I didn't ask again.

Anyway, having spent the best part of the week in the air-raid shelter, I was glad of a break. I sunbathed in the garden. I got out my drawing book and drew the church across the road from us, then the pear tree in the garden. Then Lal when she wasn't looking. And on the spur of the moment – was I bored? Does boredom sometimes make you do things you wouldn't otherwise do? In fact, is boredom useful? – whatever, I put my drawing book in my satchel and went down to the beach. It was a waste of time being shy, I thought. And hadn't I known the artist since I was little? This time I'd talk to him.

And when I did find him, it was really strange because although I've seen him year after year after year, it was as if I'd never really seen him before. He was painting near the pier. It was very hot and there was a kind of stillness about him. I suppose because he was concentrating so hard. He was wearing a straw hat, torn around the edges, a paint-stained shirt and long shorts. He had ginger hair and that pale, translucent skin (like Dottie's) that burns easily.

It was a shock, that's all I can say, the sudden ache I felt seeing the light ginger hairs on his arms and wanting to reach out and stroke him. I think I blushed just standing there looking at him. It was a good job he had his back to me. There was another painting leaning against his canvas stool and drying in the sun. It was of a child standing on a rock and looking towards the two islands you could see from Norton's beach. One of them was a bird sanctuary, though Natalie said it might well be a Left-Over Nazi hideout, the place they could storm out from. The other island disappeared at high tide. I could see the name scrawled in a corner of the canvas. HUGO KESLER, it said. I turned the name over on my tongue, kind of tasting it.

Without turning round, as if he'd just sensed me being there, Hugo said, 'I'm trying to catch the light.'

Those were his first ever words to me. Before even 'hello' or 'hi'. It stuck with me like a kind of mantra which, at the worst times of that summer and when it was all over and I was trying to make sense of it all, I'd repeat to myself, over and over. *I'm trying to catch the light.*

Then he turned round and smiled at me, tipping the straw hat back. 'And who might you be?' he asked. 'Have you come out of the sea. Are you a sea nymph or a mortal?'

'A mortal,' I said, 'and my name's Lizzie.'

Over his shoulder I could see that he'd been mixing smoky greys, whites, a whole range of blues and an unexpected pink that somehow was exactly the *right* pink to catch the kind of shine you get on the sea. There was a boy in the painting – the same one as in the picture with his name on it. He looked rather like Philip, only a mended Philip, if that makes sense, and wearing a red jersey so that, small as he was, he seemed to be the most important part of the painting.

'Well, mortal Lizzie,' said Hugo. 'Do you like painting?'

'And drawing,' I said.

'Ah, drawing! We shall need a whole afternoon to talk about drawing. And maybe I could draw *you*?'

I think I probably blushed again and then I ran off. I thought I might burst with happiness if I didn't.

But I was going back. When Natalie's note arrived, that's what I was planning. Going back to see Hugo. I'd put on my favourite skirt and top. This time I was going to show him my drawing book.

Then the note arrived. Natalie put it through our door. Perhaps she'd known where I lived all along but hadn't said. Maybe she'd posted it late at night and I hadn't heard the gate go. Or maybe she'd sent Philip. For a boy with a limp, Philip was so light on his feet that sometimes you didn't know he was there.

Lal brought the note in with the post, dancing around the breakfast table with it.

'This is for you, Lizzie-Lou,' she said.

I tried to snatch it from her but she held it up and read it out loud: '*OP Ten. P is ready. Be there . . .* Operation Ten,' she translated. 'Are we in a little gang then? Ze French Resistance movement, n'est-ce pas?'

'Leave her alone,' Mum said. 'It's just girls.'

Lal shrugged, ruffled my hair and went off to work. Paul was due home soon. Lal had gone from pale and languishing – lovelorn, as Mum called it – to semi-radiant. First thing in the morning you needed sunglasses to look at her.

Little did either of them know. I ate my breakfast fast. I knew that *OP 10* meant *our place*, which was the air-raid shelter, and that I was to be there at ten. P – for Philip – was ready. That wasn't quite so clear. Was he ready to See Left-Over Nazis? Had he actually seen one? The man with the cars perhaps, or the girl with the ring? Were there times when Philip could See and times he couldn't? How did it work?

Just the thought of the air-raid shelter on a bright sunny morning settled like a shadow on my heart. I had to shut my eyes and picture Natalie, my wild spirit, my *kindred spirit*. I pictured her as she'd been on the pier soon after we'd met, the red ribbon flying from her hair like a streamer, her strut, her grin, her crazy dares. Then I put my drawing book back in my bedroom, changed out of my favourite skirt and set off for the shelter.

It seemed even more dank and dark there than it had before. Maybe because it was such a bright and sunny morning. There were families coming across the sand hills, mums with picnic baskets and rugs, little kids running ahead with buckets and spades. I had to wait until no one was passing to duck through the door of the shelter. And then I had to wait until my eyes adjusted to the darkness and I could see Natalie and Philip waiting for me.

I could tell Natalie was angry by the way she sat there, very stiff and upright, on two old fish boxes like they were a mini throne, with Philip squatting at her feet. She kept tossing her head and refusing to look at me. I waited.

'You were doubtful,' she accused at last. 'Doubtful about Philip's dream.'

'It was just that it was – well, vague,' I protested. 'The man with the car, the girl with a ring—'

'You don't understand,' Natalie said sharply. 'Dreams, Visions, Seeings – you have to work out their meaning. It's not like someone telling you what to do. You have to interpret.'

I knew it wasn't the moment to question her but I was feeling huffy. I'd come here when I'd really wanted to see Hugo.

'So I suppose you're the grand interpreter?' I said.

'If you like,' Natalie said, as if 'grand' was what she was. Always. 'But we've brought you here to witness a Seeing.'

'I thought we had to wait,' I said nervously. 'I thought you couldn't arrange it. I thought it just . . . well, happened.'

'I have the ability to help Philip into a Seeing,' said Natalie. 'You could say I'm his mentor. We need to prepare him.'

Preparing Philip involved draping the silky shawl over his jersey and fastening it with a safety pin. Natalie had made a kind of small crown for his head out of cardboard and tinfoil. She put this on at the same time as she removed his specs, as though for this kind of Seeing, Philip wouldn't need them.

This is stupid, I thought. *It's just going to be silly*. But it wasn't. It wasn't because of how Philip changed. He stood very straight. Without his specs his face looked angelic, a pale oval in the dim light of the shelter. His rough thatch of hair, which looked as if it had never seen a comb, stuck out from the cardboard crown, the colour of early corn. I saw the pupils of his eyes getting bigger as I looked at him. The Philip I'd known until then, the loopy little boy who'd screamed with fright when Natalie and I walked out onto the rotting pier, the boy who'd hid in a corner eating baked beans out of the pan, then stuttering his dream – he'd gone. The Philip who stood there now was proud, confident, certain of himself.

'Coming into his own,' Natalie whispered. 'And now we must do the Vow.'

I was locked in now. Everything else – Lal, Hugo, my old friends Alice and Dottie – forgotten. We held hands and chanted. (Philip closed his eyes.)

'*I, Natalie Rafferty, and I, Lizzie Worthing, hereby vow undying friendship, and that we, together with Philip Rafferty, hereby pledge to rout out evil from the world, and in particular to find and expose all members of the Gestapo still lurking undercover and waiting to dominate the world, putting all Jews and their kin to death.*'

'Amen,' said Philip.

Outside I could hear all the everyday sounds – the excited voices of children running across the sand hills to the beach, a clank of bucket and spade, a mother calling a child to slow down, a faint burst of jazz from the artist's caravan – a come-out-and-play sound. Once, during our chant, a dog put his nose in through the door of the shelter, sniffed and ran away. All of it seemed a world away.

'Hold the gas mask,' said Natalie – without my noticing, she'd brought it out. 'In memory of those who died.'

We all put our hands on the mask.

'In memory of those who died,' said Philip.

'In memory of those who died,' I echoed.

Philip was crying now but his crying was odd. There was no sound to it and his face didn't move. He seemed perfectly calm apart from the tears streaming down his cheeks – almost, I thought, as if he was simply washing his eyes out, as if he had to wash the daily stuff out of his eyes before he could really See.

'Close eyes and hold hands,' Natalie instructed. Philip's hand was icy, mine sweaty, Natalie's cool.

'Now we need to dance,' she said.

'Dance?' I'd been almost in a trance, but the suggestion of dancing seemed to bring me round, as if it was just one step too far.

Natalie ignored the question in my voice, just gripped my hand more tightly. The three of us circled slowly. Natalie began a slow hum, low in her throat. Soon Philip joined in and, nudged by Natalie, so did I.

This is a weird kind of dream, I thought, *or a charade*. Then Philip began shaking. Slightly at first and then taken over by it as if it was beyond his control. His head was flung back. He jerked and shook until one last shudder went through him and then he was still, his eyes wide open but unseeing. Of us, at least.

'He's there!' whispered Natalie.

Philip raised his hands, made a shape with his fingers.

'His swastika sign!' There was triumph in Natalie's voice.

When Philip began speaking his usual stutter had gone. What had I expected? I don't know. I couldn't understand anything he said. Couldn't *see* who or what Philip spoke of in his Seeing state.

'Old, very old,' he began. 'And, oh, what a funny hat!' He laughed at this for some time. Then, 'Must get the fish,' he said. 'Shuffle, shuffle, shuffle.' He acted out an odd shuffling walk. 'Who's following me? Someone? Watch my back. Pretend to be reading.'

Philip sat on the shelter's floor and appeared to be reading an invisible newspaper because he spread it out, licking a finger to turn the pages. 'Speak to no one. Keep mum. Oh! Oh! Oh!'

With the last three 'Oh's, Philip curled up like a baby, opening his ordinary eyes – or rather, his eyes went back to normal – looked up at Natalie and said, 'Was that all right?'

Natalie rocked and cradled him, taking off the crown and shawl, stroking his head. 'You did well. You did very, very well,' she crooned.

Immediately Philip fell asleep, just as he was, curled up on the floor. Natalie covered him with the shawl and gave me a smile like a conjuror who's just performed his finest trick.

'Convinced?' she asked.

I swallowed hard. I felt all weird and shaky. And that's how my voice came out when at last I managed to speak. I couldn't deny what I'd seen, though I wanted to. I felt like someone in shock. 'Yes,' I said – and it came out in a kind of gulp. 'Yes, yes, I'm convinced. But what does it mean?'

Natalie gave me a withering look. 'I suppose you think the Oracle of Delphi was easy to understand?'

I hadn't heard of the Oracle of Delphi but then I hadn't thought of Philip as any kind of oracle. He was just a small boy. I looked at him lying there, all of eight years old, and he looked so little, so vulnerable, that I suddenly wondered if being a Seer wasn't a gift at all. If perhaps it was a great burden.

'We have to translate,' said Natalie. 'We have to use *our* eyes to translate his *Seeing*.'

Suddenly it all felt too much. I wanted to get out. Get out of the shelter and into the sunshine. It was all becoming too close, too real.

'Someone old who wears a funny hat and shuffles . . .' I said, repeating the words of Philip's Seeing. 'Maybe it's just someone Philip's seen in a comic, someone imaginary—' That's what I wanted it to be. Someone imaginary.

Natalie cut me off, slicing the air with her hand. 'I suppose you think that's funny,' she said.

'Just joking!' I said lamely.

'Well, don't. Believe me. Believe Philip. Whoever he's Seen is a LON, a Left-Over Nazi. And we'll find him.'

The Caravan
Very Sunny Morning

Dear Helena,
Many thanks for the cake. It was delicious. My new young friend, Philip, helped me eat it. I told him my sister makes the best cake in the world and as I don't think he's ever given cake at home he was more than ready to believe me.

I've made some good sketches of him and one painting. He seems to arrive at all times of the day or sometimes quite late in the evening. He's usually hungry and quite often in need of a good wash. I've made a space for him in the caravan. He's got his own small cupboard, a Mickey Mouse mug and a box of wax crayons. He loves the caravan, either being inside, when I set the table up and give him some paper, or outside, sitting with me on the step. One glimpse of that wild sister of his, and either he limps away as quick as he can or he hides under the bunk bed.

I've begun to think that he might be a bit fey or psychic. Anyway, he's happiest inside the caravan, sometimes tucked up on the bunk bed with an old blanket and one of my sketchbooks to look at. I hear him talking to himself – he doesn't stutter when he's talking to himself – and it's as though he's seeing through the picture he's looking at to the story that's behind it. It's hard to explain. He looked at an old drawing I'd done of Dr Jacobs – you know, the one who got me through the worst of the breakdown – and he kept patting the picture and saying, 'Make you better, make you better.' There's nothing in the drawing that tells you this is a doctor. It could be anyone.

I'm probably reading far too much into this. Maybe Philip is hoping that I'll make him better. Make his limp better. His stutter.

His eyesight. Goodness knows where he got the specs that he wears. One way or another, although that wild sister of his seems to guard him, I'm not at all sure she actually looks after him. Or that anyone does.

Send more cake! I'm sure that would help.

Love as always,
Hugo

Chapter 8
Stalking

The first LON that Philip put the finger on was Sam Dingle at the garage.

By the first week of August we'd seriously begun what Natalie called our *Lonnie Watch*. She insisted that we start our daily patrol of Norton in the air-raid shelter. Philip had to be prepared, keyed up, ready to see inside people, 'spot the swastika', as Natalie put it.

We had to repeat the Vow. Then Natalie would imitate the air-raid siren – louder and louder whoops until Philip put his fingers in his ears. We did some marching up and down the shelter, chanting, 'Rout them out! Rout them out! Last of the Nazis, rout them out!'

By then Philip would be all pop-eyed and trembling. Natalie would put her hands on his shoulders like she was a priestess giving him a blessing. 'He's ready,' she'd say, and off we'd go.

We did a circuit of Norton, starting at the top of the village, which was the boring end, full of seriously large houses (like mine) with lace curtains at the windows and big trees in the front gardens, houses heavy with respectability. No one in these houses, I thought, would consider committing even a minor crime, let alone be working for the Nazis. But that, said Natalie, was the whole point. LONs lurked in places you would never guess they lurked in.

On the corner where the big houses stopped was the cottage hospital. It had a veranda and sometimes one or two patients would be wheeled out onto it, still in their beds. 'A good lookout post,' said Natalie.

'No one's going to *pretend* to be ill!' I said. It was one of those moments when I thought maybe she was crazy.

But Natalie just raised her eyebrows at me. 'You've such a small imagination,' she said. It's very crushing to think your imagination is small.

We went on down what was called Market Street (though as far as I know there's never been a market there), past the usual queue at the post office, which also did newspapers, past The Anchor, where the old sailors sat outside on a bench, smoking their pipes. ('Poor old things,' said Natalie. 'They could be caught napping if the LONs attack.') On Wednesdays and Fridays there was another queue at the fish cart on the corner where the woman we called Mrs Kipper would chop the heads off your plaice and slap and wrap its slit body in newspaper.

If we were doing an afternoon patrol we'd see a gang from our school going into the newly opened coffee bar. Sometimes I'd see Alice among them. She'd look over at me and I'd feel a kind of pang, remembering how it had been when she was my best friend. How *easy* it had been. Sometimes I tried a smile and a half-wave, but Alice just looked away and Natalie tugged at my arm. 'Ignore them!' she said. 'We've work to do.'

Natalie never let me forget that peace was an illusion, that evil was all around us, waiting, hidden.

Our route took in all the narrow streets of prim terraced houses that led down to the railway station, and the roads down to the sea where the houses looked weatherbeaten, and where boats leaned on blocks in the gardens so that you knew it was the boats that were important and the houses a bit irrelevant. One way or another we stalked Norton from the library at the top, past three churches, two pubs, the shops and the cottage hospital.

Sam Dingle was a tall, very thin man, as flat and straight as the petrol pumps he attended. He wore a flat cap, as if to stop himself growing any further. He'd been at the garage for so long that he looked as if he might turn into a petrol pump and all you had to do was take off his cap and find the petrol pump's nozzle inside his head. Mum used to say that Sam Dingle was 'sixpence short of a shilling' which, when I was little, I thought meant that he was very poor so I offered him my pocket money.

The garage was at the top end of Market Street. There was a bench opposite. It was known as the Mary Robbins bench because it had FOR MARY ROBBINS WHO LOVED THIS PLACE written across the back of it. It had probably been there before the garage, because who would love to sit facing a smelly garage? Anyway, that's where we sat, mid patrol, Natalie, Philip and me, because I'd just spent the last of my pocket money on three ice-cream cornets. We'd finished them when Philip began shaking all over. His face scrunched up and his eyes rolled back in his head.

'This is a Seeing!' said Natalie. 'This is his trance.'

Once the shaking stopped, Philip stood up. His eyes were closed. I remembered how he'd been in the air-raid shelter, suddenly confident, his stutter gone, a certainty about him as if, I thought this time, he was eighty, not eight.

When he opened his eyes he simply pointed his finger straight at Sam Dingle. 'That one!' he said.

Natalie and I spoke simultaneously.

'The man with the cars!' she said.

'The man in his dream,' I said.

Philip collapsed against Natalie. She put her arms around him and held him tight as tight until some colour came back into his cheeks and he seemed back to normal – whatever normal was. Natalie was triumphant.

As for me, it was as if Philip's Seeing had changed my own seeing. Why had I thought him friendly and harmless before? Silly old Sam Dingle with a head like a petrol pump. No. His face, I now saw, was sharp as a fox's. He had mean little eyes. He walked stiffly, like a soldier. He wore heavy boots. Jackboots?

Natalie planned our campaign. Back in the air-raid shelter we wrote anonymous letters to Sam. We used a thick black pen and wrote in capitals. One letter said WE KNOW WHO YOU ARE, and had a swastika drawn at the bottom. A second said NO MORE NAZIS. A third, YOU'RE NOT WANTED HERE, with another swastika. We took it in turns to post the letters under the door of the booth where people paid for their petrol and where Sam ate his sandwiches at lunch time. We did it when the garage closed at five-thirty. One day we drew a big swastika and stuck it on one of the petrol pumps.

After that we made a point of sitting on the Mary Robbins bench and watching. Sam saw us but I don't think he ever suspected us. Natalie enjoyed walking past the garage and saying hello to him, nudging Philip in the ribs and putting on a falsely posh voice. 'Say hello nicely, Philip,' she'd say. I think Sam actually liked us. Once he dug some toffees out of his pocket and gave them to Philip. I think he'd bought them specially. But Natalie made Philip throw them away.

Day by day we watched Sam growing jumpier and, if possible, thinner. He didn't stand by the pumps like he used to do, greeting people and waiting for customers. He lurked inside, and when he did come out he looked all around first. He didn't chat to the customers any more either. Natalie said it was guilt that was doing it to him and that he knew he'd been found out. She said one LON would lead to another. And another and another.

By the end of the month Sam had retired from the garage and moved house. Natalie put his name down in her *Messages* notebook and then drew a line through it to show he'd been eliminated.

Mum said it was odd, Sam Dingle moving when he'd lived all his life in Norton. But then she said that perhaps he'd welcome a change. 'Perhaps he's had enough,' she said, as if she knew what it felt like to have had enough – which surprised me because mostly Mum irritatingly insisted on being happy. Anyway, 'A change of scene. Pastures new,' Mum continued. I couldn't imagine Sam in pastures new with cows instead of cars. I thought he'd miss his petrol pumps.

In fact, it was funny, but once he'd gone, I missed him too. It was as if in my mind's eye – and how odd was that? A mind having an eye – well, as if when I thought about him, my memory remembered him as he had been, as I'd seen him before Philip had pointed the finger at him and said, 'That one!'

It made me feel a bit queasy, as if I couldn't rely on my eyes any more. They seemed intent on playing tricks on me. I suppose some tricks can be nice, like when you look at a cloud and it looks like the head of an elephant or you pick up a stick and you can see the shape of a cat in it. But this was different. This was not knowing which was true, the old Sam Dingle who'd refused my pocket money or the Sam Dingle who was secretly a LON.

Maybe that was why, when I had what I thought of as my 'translating' moment, I didn't immediately tell Natalie.

Natalie's Diary

Thursday or maybe Friday

Sam Dingle. LON 1, Norton 1953. Dispatched. Good riddance to bad rubbish (in future GRBR).

Got to make sure Philip's clear. He was rambling in his sleep about Ma's men and Nazi men. Did Sam Dingle ever visit Ma? Think not but can't be certain.

NB to Self. In future stay awake as late as poss.

Feeling like I did in London. Triumph first then really, really empty as if I haven't eaten for weeks. How many LONs does it take to make up for one da? A hundred? A thousand? When will I know I'm done? Worried Lizzie won't stick with me unless I keep her scared. You can keep people if you scare them. I've found that out. You lose them if you love them. That's what I think.

Another row with Ma. The rent's gone on gin. Told the man we'd be sure to have it for next week. Him, all snidey, 'Tell your ma there's other ways of paying.'

Expect she will. Told her I wish she'd died, not Da.

Why is she always so nasty about him? Saying he was no good. Saying there were other women. Saying even if he hadn't gone in the RAF he'd have left us anyway. She's lying. She lies about everything. I don't believe any of it.

She says I can't remember, but I do. I remember riding on his shoulders. I remember him singing me to sleep. His voice rough but gentle.

Oh, he could sing all right, Ma says. Sing for his supper.

(What does that mean?) About the only thing he could do, she says. And die, I think. He could do that. For his country. For us.

NB to Self. Find out where Philip keeps going off to. I think it's that artist in the yellow caravan. I think Lizzie goes there too. They don't tell me. He's a threat.

Chapter 9

A Third Eye

It happened when I was out shopping with Lal. Mum was ill. Lal had taken time off work to look after Dad and me, though I told her I was quite capable of looking after everyone. Mum had a bad tummy bug – gastro-something-or-other. The doctor said she was to stay in bed. Nothing to eat. Just fluids. She was an awful patient. Kept calling downstairs to check on us, Lal and me. Had we mopped the kitchen floor? Remembered to bank up the Aga with anthracite? Had Dad got a clean shirt for tomorrow?

'Rest! Sleep!' Lal told her. 'We're going to get the shopping done. We'll get you some Lucozade.'

Mum flopped back on her pillows. You could tell she hadn't the energy to argue much. That was a relief!

Anyway, it was nice being out with Lal, even if she did go on and on about Paul: round about now he'll be leaving Hong Kong, and there's only so many days, hours and minutes before he's home, etc., etc. I carried the shopping basket. Lal carried the money.

We'd done all the food shopping and were ready for home when Lal spotted the florist's. 'Just a quick look,' she said. 'I need ideas for my bouquet and your posy.'

'I don't want a posy . . .' I began. But Lal hooked her arm in mine and marched me towards the florist's. It was then that I saw him. Mr Oliver.

Of course, I'd often seen him. Mr Oliver was one of Norton's 'characters', along with the old maids in the café and the witch in the sweetie shop and the man who loved babies and, I suppose, the artist. My Hugo.

Mr Oliver had a kind of furtive, shuffling walk. Summer and winter he dressed the same – an old mac, a grey woollen scarf and a funny tasselled hat. He was what Mum called *regular in his habits*, which meant that any day of the week you could see him doing exactly the same thing. The post office to buy a single airmail letter and a newspaper. Then to the fish cart to buy a kipper or filleted plaice. (That's when you heard him speak and knew he wasn't English.) After that, whatever the weather, he walked along the promenade to a seat in one of the shelters – always the same one – for an hour, maybe two, and he just looked out at the sea, his bag of fish and his unopened newspaper beside him. Then off he went home with that same furtive shuffle as if once upon a time he'd done something very, very wrong.

Shuffle, shuffle, shuffle. Must get the fish!

I stopped dead in front of the florist's.

Philip's Seeing flashed before me, as if – madly – I was seeing and hearing it myself! Translating it. Making sense of it. It wasn't the shuffle that did it, it was Philip's final *Oh! Oh! Oh!* which, at the time, hadn't meant anything at all but now, plain as daylight, plain as Lal's arm in mine, meant O for Oliver.

Was Mr Oliver a Left-Over Nazi? Or worse, one of the ones we were meant to be hunting out? The translation process suddenly made everything he did acutely suspicious. I think I briefly went into some kind of trance, because the next thing I knew was Lal asking me if I was OK.

'You've gone white as a sheet,' she said. 'Is it the lilies? They're meant to be for funerals.' I hadn't even noticed the large tub of lilies outside the florist's shop.

'I'm fine,' I said. 'Fine.'

'I hope you're not catching something,' Lal said, 'like Mum's bug.'

I'd given myself such a fright I was almost ready to blurt it all out, to tell Lal about the Left-Over Nazis, about the Vow, the quest, Philip's Seeings. But then, somehow, it was as if Natalie was standing beside me, fierce and certain, telling me that evil could never stop.

We were inside the florist's shop now. Lal was back on weddings.

'Delphiniums,' she was saying. 'I love delphiniums. They could be my "something blue", couldn't they?'

She was so happy, so unafraid. And she was going away. Natalie wasn't.

I allowed her to talk me into a bridesmaid's posy and I didn't tell her about the LONs or the Vow or the plans we made in the air-raid shelter.

Nor did I tell Natalie about Mr Oliver. I couldn't face it. It was one thing, Philip pointing the finger at Sam Dingle. I didn't want to be the one who pointed the finger at Mr Oliver. So I avoided Natalie all week. I had to look after Mum, I said, which was partly true, although actually Lal was the one doing that. Me? I was with Hugo.

'We shall need a whole afternoon to talk about drawing' – that's what he'd said. And it hadn't happened because Natalie's note had arrived demanding an urgent meeting in the air-raid shelter. Some days it felt as if Natalie was always demanding something.

Like my entire life! And it wasn't as if I was betraying her, going to see Hugo; it was almost as if I couldn't help myself. As if the darkness of the air-raid shelter, the hours spent writing anonymous warnings for Sam Dingle, blackening swastikas, had got right into me, like damp gets into a house. I needed light, sunshine, a yellow caravan, Hugo.

'It's the sea nymph again,' Hugo said. 'I thought you'd gone off into the ocean like the Little Mermaid. She lost her tongue, you know. Have you lost yours?'

'No,' I said. 'And my name's Lizzie. You said we could talk about drawing . . .'

Hugo had brought his canvas stool out in front of the caravan. He had his sketchbook on his knees. I perched on the sea wall and felt suddenly happy. Happy just to watch. To watch the sun glinting on the pale ginger of his arms, to watch the way he screwed up his eyes when he looked into the distance. Most of all I liked seeing the magic lines the piece of charcoal made on the paper, lines that all of a sudden became something – a boat, seaweed on some rocks, a gull.

'We could talk about drawing, or I could draw you,' Hugo said. 'Which shall it be?'

'Can I see some paintings first?' I asked.

Hugo laughed. 'You mean we've only just met and you're not quite ready to be drawn. Come! I'll show you.'

Inside the caravan it was hot. And though there were dead things – birds' feathers, a fish skeleton, empty mussel shells, part of a gull's skull – the place seemed alive with energy. It was the canvases full of colour that did it and the charcoal sketches pinned on a board above the window, as full of movement as if Hugo had just let his hand take over and go where it wanted. Some of the sketches were of people I recognized – Mrs Kipper, the fish-cart woman, one of the old sailors from outside The Anchor, Jim Armitage who delivered newspapers on his bike.

Then there was all the homely stuff – a kettle and mugs, books and brushes, tins of beans, the stack of driftwood for the campfires Hugo cooked on.

Hugo began pulling out paintings to show me. The first one was of children on a beach. They looked alike, as if they might be brother and sister, yet they were also strangers. The girl seemed to have a shadow behind her as if there was a third child missing. The boy was making something out of sand but his spade was dipping into blood.

Hugo stood back, watching me watching. 'Well?'

'Well,' I said, 'it's – er – very colourful!'

'Now say what you really think.'

'It's . . . it's . . . uncomfortable,' I said.

'Good! What about this one?'

This one was easier because I recognized the scene Hugo had painted. It was the line of houses along the promenade and one of the shelters – possibly the one Mr Oliver sat in with his fish and his newspaper. What was strange about this picture was that I saw things I hadn't seen before. A roof had grown a weathervane, one house had a balcony added with a towel slung over it, another had a window shaped like a slit for arrows, yet another had ribbons of ivy running down over the front windows so no one inside could possibly see out. The painting made you wonder about the people living in these houses, made you wonder about what you *couldn't* see. It was odd. And clever. The more I looked, the more I began to see other things Hugo had added – a snake wound round a chimneypot, a garden gnome with a magic wand, a creature that looked like a monkey sitting cross-legged on a postbox – it made me laugh.

'There never was a monkey,' I said. 'Or a snake. You didn't see them.'

'I did with my other eye,' said Hugo, so seriously that for a moment I found myself staring at his forehead, looking for a third eye.

Hugo tilted my face towards the light from the open door. 'An old face,' he said. 'And good bones. Do you draw? Do you paint? What do you do, Lizzie sea nymph?'

'Sometimes,' I said. 'Sometimes I draw.'

'Secretly, isn't it?' said Hugo.

'How did you know?'

'Saw it in your eyes!'

'You never!'

'No, I never. It was a guess. But a right one, yes?'

'Yes.'

'Come and see me again. Often. Bring your drawings. And let me draw you. Is that a deal?'

He was holding out his hand. I had a really silly desire to kiss it.

'A deal!' I said, and we shook on it.

I think maybe I floated out of the caravan feeling light-headed and light-hearted.

It was only when I was halfway up the slipway, heading towards the road, that I looked back and saw Philip making for the caravan. When he saw Hugo he did his best to run. I stopped. Watched as Hugo opened his arms, lifted Philip off his feet and swung him round. Philip was laughing. They were both laughing.

The light-hearted feeling went like a cloud coming over the sun. *Natalie's not going to like this,* I thought. Then, *Does she need to know?*

Chapter 10

Roll-mop Herrings

'Poisoned,' said Natalie. 'That would explain it.'

We were at The Baths. Natalie had got bored with our LON patrol and we were having a morning off. Or so I thought.

'But why?' I asked. 'Why Mum?'

'Until the LONs are strong enough to take over, they like to try and exterminate people one by one. Jewish people, that is. Poisoning. It could seem like an epidemic.'

I hated the word *exterminate*. It made me think of beetles being crushed underfoot. Part of me thought Mum was altogether too plump and cheery to be exterminated by anyone and that Natalie was being ridiculous. Then, as always, came that clutch at my heart, that awful question: *What if she's right?*

'The doctor's been to see her,' I said. 'She'd know if she'd been poisoned.'

Natalie shrugged. Doctors ranked with teachers and policemen for Natalie. They weren't to be trusted.

'Where does she shop?' she asked.

'Mason's,' I said. 'She has an order delivered every week. But she eats everything that we eat – Dad, Lal and me – or almost . . .'

'Almost?'

I'd suddenly remembered that Mum was the only one who drank coffee and ate roll-mop herrings, which the rest of us couldn't even bear the look of.

'Almost,' I muttered.

'We'll check it out,' Natalie said briskly. She sounded as pleased as a detective who's just been handed a really good clue.

Every morning for the next week we went into Mason's.

Philip was dragged along with us. I badly wanted to ask him about Hugo but I didn't think he'd want Natalie to know. If Natalie was possessive of me, she was even more so of Philip. As soon as our visit to Mason's was over – and it never took long – Philip was off.

'I don't know what's got into him,' Natalie said crossly. 'But I'll find out.'

'Maybe he just doesn't want to hang about with us,' I said. 'Maybe he's found a friend.' That was as near as I got to telling her about Hugo.

'He doesn't need a friend,' Natalie said. 'He's got me. And you,' she added.

There wasn't much we could afford to buy at Mason's, but there was a small counter of cheap sweets, and often we'd spend our time pretending we were trying to decide on dolly mixtures or jelly babies or a packet of fizz, until Mrs Mason said, 'Now then, you've had quite long enough. What d'you want?'

Then Natalie would smile very sweetly and say, 'Nothing today, thank you, Mrs Mason.'

There was a Mr Mason who worked out the back, mostly packing boxes for delivery in the van, and a young girl, Maisie. It was Maisie who Philip pointed the finger at. It was the fifth morning and we'd almost given up. Natalie and I had nearly convinced ourselves that Mrs Mason was a LON capable of poisoning Mum's roll-mop herrings or her jar of coffee. She was a large, grim lady who bullied both Mr Mason and Maisie. We watched her like hawks.

But Maisie Lewis was a plump, pretty girl of no more than eighteen. She had a ponytail and a new and shiny engagement ring. Her fiancé was Bob Liddle, who lived down near the station and worked in the ironmonger's.

Philip went through the same Seeing ritual – the sudden shaking, the screwed-up face and rolled-back eyes. We had to bundle him out of the shop and it was only when we were outside that he pointed through the window at Maisie.

'She can't be!' I said. 'She can't be a LON. She's too young and she looks really sweet.'

'You don't get it, do you?' said Natalie, exasperated. 'Finding LONs is like finding criminals. You don't expect a murderer to look like a murderer, do you?'

'I've no idea what a murderer looks like,' I said. I could hear my voice going all squeaky as it does when I'm nervous or scared.

'Think of the boy next door or some nice little old lady,' said Natalie. 'Someone who looks really, really innocent. That's probably the murderer. Anyway,' she continued, 'didn't you know that lots of women fell in love with Hitler? Maybe Maisie was one of them.'

I said I hadn't known about women falling in love with Hitler and I thought Maisie was in love with Bob Liddle, not Hitler.

'Just a cover-up,' said Natalie. 'I expect she's been co-opted and bribed just because she looks so young and pretty.'

We didn't go for Maisie directly. We went for Bob Liddle. Bob Liddle was quite a lot older than Maisie. Mum said he was a bit of a loner and maybe Maisie would cheer him up. It was Bob who got the notes saying YOUR GIRL LOVES THE NAZIS and ASK HER WHAT SHE'S PAID and WHO WANTS NAZI BABIES?

The next time we went into Mason's, Maisie was looking red-eyed and without her engagement ring. Soon after that she went and got a job in town.

'She could still be a LON,' I said. 'Only working in town.'

'No,' said Natalie. 'Not now she's been discovered. She won't be able to continue.' And she wrote Maisie's name in the *Messages* book and put the usual black line through it.

Sometimes I saw Bob Liddle wandering about the village, a loner again, and I remembered how cheerful he'd looked, arm in arm with Maisie and maybe sharing a joke. She'd be giggling. He was too old to giggle, but he'd be smiling. Still, I tried to remember what Natalie had said which was that Bob would thank us one day and we'd saved him from a terrible marriage.

Even with Maisie gone and Mum better – in fact, Mum full of mother-of-the-bride bounce again – I wasn't a hundred per cent certain about the groceries we got from Mason's. I tried drinking the remains of Mum's coffee when she'd popped out to the kitchen and I made myself try a disgusting roll-mop herring. I wasn't sick, and when, after a few days, I was still alive, I reasoned Mum was safe.

And then I pushed Maisie and the poisoning to the back of my mind because soon after that we began tracking Mr Oliver.

The Caravan
Eye of the storm

Dear Helena,
There's a summer storm. I've wrapped myself in my old dressing gown, made myself a mug of tea and I'm sitting here writing to you and trying not to get too bothered by the thunder and lightning. It's quite something being in a caravan with the rain drilling on the roof and the lightning flashing at the window like a spotlight trying to find me. The wind's up, making the sand fly. It stings if you're out there. So I'm not. Every roll of thunder seems to make the caravan shudder.

Needless to say, there's not a soul on the beach. I was out soon after dawn painting the sky because it was so dark and ominous. It hung over the sea like it was frowning and the sea was all stirred up and restless. Coming to the boil, I thought. A few last fishing boats struggled in just before dawn – glad to get back home, by the look of the men, their oilskins dripping. Last night was the sort of night that brings the lifeboat out.

News. I've a second sitter. Name of Lizzie. (She's the Dreamy One. Also keen on drawing.) We've made a deal, Lizzie and I. I shall teach her some colours and perspective and she will let me draw her. She's shy. Pretty in a very English way. Actually I was expecting her today, but no one would come out in a storm like this.

So now I've two of the trio. Philip and Lizzie. What I badly want is to draw – paint – all three together as I saw them when I arrived. The three of them together tells some kind of story. It's hard to explain. It's something to do with friendship, being pals, best of best friends. With Philip, the little brother, as the important extra. For the moment I'm happy enough to be drawing Philip and Lizzie. Neither, as yet, knows about the visits of the other. No, I'm not trying to make a mystery where there isn't one. It's just that when the Wild One appears, Philip either hides or runs off while Lizzie goes all tense and won't come out of the caravan. Neither of them will talk about her.

Fanciful to think they're in her power – the Wild One's, that is. Though if you saw her you'd perhaps understand. On her own she struts past me. Sometimes she gives me such a fierce look I half expect her to pull a gun from the pocket of her shorts and shoot me down! What really bugs me is that if there is such a creature as a muse, I think she might be mine. Why can't it be Lizzie or Philip, or you, for that matter? I think the Wild One is not only wild but possibly cruel. Is 'cruel' too harsh a word? I don't know. What I do know is that if I asked to paint her now, she'd either snub me or laugh at me. I have to wait. Wait for the right moment.

Also I'm worried about Philip. Some days he's just like any little boy. Then he'll turn up late at night. It's almost dark and it's like a wee ghost appearing, he looks so pale and underfed. I gave him scrambled eggs on toast and walked him home, so now at least I know where he lives. Caught a glimpse of his mother who I suspect is a prostitute. No sign of the sister, the Wild One. Expect she's up in her bedroom casting spells!

Maybe she's cast one on Philip. Lately when he's got out the wax crayons he draws these awful swastikas. I ask him what he knows about the war and he just shakes his head and says, 'Bastard uncles, bastard uncles!' What's that about? I had to tell him about Jo because whenever he looks at a picture of you – I discover I have rather a lot! – he says, 'B-but b-brother, b-brother?'

'You're right,' I told him at last. 'I did have a brother. His name was Jo, but he died.' I couldn't bring myself to tell him the whole story – the Gestapo storming the house, dragging off Ma and Pa, Uncle Reuben shoving you and me into the big cupboard under the stairs and trying

to drag Jo too. Only Jo wouldn't let go of Ma. All three of them taken to Auschwitz. I thought Philip had enough to cope with with the bastard uncles – whoever they are. And I've no idea what the swastikas mean to him.

'Sad,' said Philip. 'Poor Jo,' and he leaned over and kissed my cheek. It was all I could do not to cry.

Well, apart from swastikas, the only other thing Philip draws is fire.

Whole pages of flames. Red, yellow, orange. He puts the crayon between his thumb and forefinger and scrubs on the paper really fiercely.

I try to get him to draw other things – shells, pebbles, a nice curly piece of seaweed – but he'll have none of it. Maybe he just likes the colours red, yellow, orange.

'Why all these flames, Philip?' I ask him and he just shakes his head and says, 'Poor Philip, poor Philip.'

'Poor Philip, my eye!' I tell him and give him a tickle. Or a doughnut. Or both.

In case you think I've forgotten, I haven't. I know Derek's waiting for more portraits for the next exhibition. I'm not completely taken over by the children, though I might be if they were around enough. No. I've done the fish woman – the one who has a cart in Market Street. And I've a new portrait on the go – a lonely old codger called Hans Oliver. He doesn't speak much English. I found him on the prom eating fish and chips. So now I go along there to draw him. He's not exactly keen but I think he's quite glad of some company.

I'll try to finish his portrait. I have it in mind to bring some new ones up to town for Derek. What would you say if perhaps I brought Philip with me? Suppose I'd have to get his mother to agree, though my impression is she'd be glad to get rid of him. What d'you think? A good idea?

And no, I'm not getting too involved or too wound up, as you put it. The sea puts me straight. Calms me down. Just waking up to it every morning – even when it's drawn far out and is just a line against the sky – I don't mind. I think it's something to do with the fact that it's always changing and yet always the same.

Ah! The storm's over and, would you believe, here's Lizzie. Looking rather like a drowned rat. Must go.

Love as always,

Hugo

Natalie's Diary

Who cares?

They think I don't know, but I do. I've got his name. He was inside the caravan and he'd left a painting out on the easel. Maybe it was drying. I could have done something to it there and then. As a kind of warning. But I didn't. Maybe that can be later. I just got his name. It's Hugo Kesler. I think that's a German name. He could be a LON.

It matters, getting a name. I found that out in London. It never worked, Philip putting the finger on someone, unless we had a name. I don't know why. Inside the concentration camps and the prisoner-of-war camps you were just a number. I've read that. Da would have been just a number. If you don't hang onto your name, you're done for.

How has he got to them? Lizzie's got a crush! Lizzie's got a crush! Lizzie's got a crush! It's not fair. I'll tell her she can't be a kindred spirit if she's going to get soppy and get a crush.

NB to Self. It is important to control all soppy emotions.

I've got to sort Philip out. He must go on Seeing – proper Seeing – for us. He's done this before. In London. It was the man who sold newspapers. P used to sit beside him for hours! Any half kindly man – and that seems to be any man who doesn't visit Ma – and he thinks he's found a daddy. It's pathetic. I'll tell him. I'll tell him even if I have to slap some sense into him.

We need to find the next LON. Lizzie's too dreamy. Wanders off in her head. If we have another LON she'll be OK. I need to keep them both close.

I am so very tired. My dreams are worse than Philip's. I don't tell. When I have one of the bad dreams I clench my fists and I rock. Rocking helps. It's the price for being chosen. Da's chosen me even if he works through Philip. The Jews were chosen. Being chosen always means suffering. Great people suffer.

We've got mice in the kitchen. I think it's mice. Could be rats. When I went for water last night I heard this scampering. Saw a tail.

I don't know why we've got a fridge. There's hardly ever anything in it. Tonight not even baked beans. P and I had bread and marg. Ma was out. She's still out. Better that than the men coming here.

I hate the woman next door. Always looking at us in that sneery way. Maybe her man's a LON. He's got mean eyes.

NB to Self. Get P to look him over.

Lizzie's got a new skirt and one of those net petticoats that make it stick out. And a wasp waist belt. She says they're not for every day. They're for 'best'. Who has a 'best'? I've got a 'worst'.

Chapter 11

Through the Letter Box

It was easy to stalk Mr Oliver. He lived alone in a house at the edge of the village. The house stood by itself with nothing but big overgrown bushes at the back of it and a narrow track at the front.

It didn't take us long to know his routine by heart. There we were at the top of the track when he came out of the house at ten past ten on the dot. And there we were waiting and watching when he shuffled up Market Street and went into the post office. We were still waiting for him when he came out with his newspaper and we sauntered behind him as he scuttled on to the fish cart. That was when we knew he didn't speak English because he always pointed to the fish he wanted and said something that sounded like 'Danka'. Sometimes we ran ahead to the shelter on the promenade, where he sat with his parcel of fish by his side, staring out to sea. We'd chant, '*Danka danka danka!*' and peer in through the windows of the shelter, pulling faces. Sometimes Natalie did cartwheels in front of him.

Well, that was the beginning.

Mr Oliver wasn't my fault. I hadn't told Natalie about how

I'd 'translated' Philip's dream. About that moment with Lal when Philip's 'Oh! Oh! Oh!' clicked in my head as O for Oliver. I didn't need to tell. Philip put the finger on him.

We were sitting at the bus stop as if we were waiting for a bus, though about three buses had gone by so anyone watching us might have guessed that's not what we were there for. And there was Mr Oliver in his old mac and funny tasselled hat, shuffling down Market Street, head bent in that way he had as if he didn't want to look at anyone or anyone to look at him.

'Regular as clockwork,' Mum used to say of Mr Oliver, 'and never talks to anyone. Maybe he's shy. He looks a bit mysterious.' Then she always added, 'Well, looks aren't everything. You can't tell a book by its cover.' Mum has a boring cliché about everything.

Watching Mr Oliver go into the post office then on to the fish cart, I found it really hard *not* to say anything to Natalie. And maybe that showed in my face because just when I thought she had hardly noticed Mr Oliver, she said, 'Philip's had another message from our father.' She nudged Philip in the ribs. 'Go on, tell,' she said.

'S-s-seen him,' said Philip, pointing at Mr Oliver. 'That one.'

'And . . .' prompted Natalie. 'The swastika. Remember?'

'Swastika on his heart,' said Philip.

If only Mr Oliver hadn't looked quite so suspicious! So furtive (Mum again). So unsmiling. Once when we were buying a bag of chips to share, he pushed past us with something like a snarl and almost knocked Philip over.

I couldn't bring myself to question Philip's dream. Hadn't I watched him when he'd been taken over by a Seeing? He didn't even seem bright enough to tell a lie, though later, much later, I wondered just how many dreams or Seeings were – well, what word could I put to it? – *prompted* by Natalie?

At first Mr Oliver seemed determined to ignore us. He wasn't going to change his habits for us, that was clear. Some days we took to playing a loud game of hopscotch in front of him when he sat in the shelter, Natalie throwing her stone and shouting, 'Achtung!' Then we'd follow him all the way home, Philip doing a limping dance, then trying to imitate Mr Oliver's shuffle.

Once, Mr Oliver turned on him, got Philip by the shoulders and shook him. Hard. It was a big mistake. More dreams followed. More urgent instructions from poor dead Mr Rafferty.

'Sam Dingle and Maisie – just minor LONs,' Natalie said. 'Mr Oliver's important. He's probably the leader of a cell.'

'A cell?'

'The local group. He'll be the one receiving instructions about the uprising.'

I didn't dare ask where Mr Oliver would be receiving instructions *from.* I was already finding it hard to sleep at night.

'But what are we meant to do with him?' I asked. We were in the air-raid shelter. Natalie said we needed to renew our Vow. She said it would 'Strengthen Our Resolve'. She said that as if it was all in capital letters and she'd read it somewhere.

'Mr Oliver,' I said again. 'What are we meant to do with him?'

'He'll go,' said Natalie. 'He'll slink off in the night. Or he'll get orders to leave. They have ways of dealing with one of their own when he fails. But we mustn't give up. We've got to keep showing him we know.'

'R-rout them out! R-rout them out!' Philip chanted. Doing the Vow always got him going again. Maybe that's why Natalie insisted we did it.

'Yes!' she said, punching Philip on the arm.

Routing Mr Oliver out became – well, it became a kind of

thrilling game that we didn't know how to stop.

Natalie had found an old linen coat. It was silk lined but the lining was torn. She patched it with old pieces of cloth on which she'd inked swastikas. Now, whenever he turned to look at us, Natalie flashed open the coat. Not that he wanted to turn and look at us. He tried to ignore us and hurry on – shuffle on. But he couldn't help himself. We knew we were winning when he tried to change the time he left his house or when he took just a slightly different route or when, although he still went to the shelter on the promenade with his fish and his newspaper, he couldn't sit still for long. Whatever he did, he couldn't shake us off. Something was in us as if it had been waiting inside us, as if all the stories we'd heard about the war had got into our bones, our blood.

We became brazen, wild enough to follow Mr Oliver down the track to his house, then right down his path. We peered in at the front window. Made faces at him. Mouthed, *Nazi! Nazi! Nazi! Go home to Germany!*

Mr Oliver's front room didn't have much furniture. It was dark and very tidy. There was a tiled fireplace with a two-bar electric fire, one armchair with wooden arms and a shelf of books. 'They're probably German,' Natalie said. There was a desk in the window with a neat stack of notebooks – 'Nazi plans,' Natalie said – a tray of pens and pencils and a small radio. Mr Oliver drew the thin curtains and turned up his radio but we knew he could see our shadows and we made sure our chanting was loud enough for him to hear. Besides, we were there again the next day and the next day and the next. Either we waited just beyond the path to his house, or on the corner at the top of the track. It was fun to surprise him. Just to make him jump a little.

Then one morning he didn't appear.

It was raining but we waited at the top of the track. No Mr Oliver. We waited until Philip began snivelling that the rain was going down the back of his neck and his shoes leaked. So although the track got muddy in the rain, we walked down to Mr Oliver's house. The curtains were still drawn and the radio was silent.

'We know you're in there!' Natalie shouted through the letter box. There was no response. We trudged back to the air-raid shelter to discuss it.

'Maybe he's ill,' I said.

'More likely he's getting in touch with Headquarters,' said Natalie. 'Knows we've found him out.'

Natalie always spoke of Headquarters as if she knew exactly where it was, as if she might have visited it or, at the very least, seen it marked on a map. I never asked her exactly where it was. Headquarters was just a place you believed in. Morning after morning, though we sat waiting on the Mary-Robbins-who-loved-this-place bench or lurked by Mrs Kipper's fish cart or idled innocently along the prom past Mr Oliver's favourite shelter, there was no sign of Mr Oliver. It was Philip who voiced what Natalie and I were thinking but didn't dare say.

'Dead,' said Philip, matter-of-factly. 'Mr Oliver. Dead and gone.'

Was that a guess or a dream or a Seeing?

And if Philip was right, was it possible to frighten the life out of someone? Was that what we'd done?

Chapter 12
GRBR

It was only when I was in the caravan with Hugo for a short hour – maybe less – that I could stop thinking about Mr Oliver.

Hugo had begun giving me drawing lessons. He'd set up a still life for me and lay out pencils or charcoal. We'd talk about angles and focus and how one shape balanced another. Or didn't. We'd talk about looking. I was allowed to clean the paintbrushes, tidy up, or occasionally help prepare and stretch a canvas.

Also I'd begun sitting for him. At first that had been really strange. Hugo sat me on the canvas stool, stood in front of me and then, with his eyes closed, felt all round my head and face as if he was memorizing me. I shut my eyes. *A person's bones are what matters*, Hugo had said, so I tried concentrating on my bones – nose, cheek, chin – while his hands moved so tenderly over my head and face that I couldn't help feeling that somehow or other he was *seeing* me through his fingers. He kept grunting, as if telling himself what his fingers had found. The whole business did nothing for my hair, which I always washed and tried to make really nice before I went to the caravan, but which very soon was all messed up.

'Don't move! Don't twitch!' Hugo ordered, so I sat as still and twitchless as I could, though from my neck to my toes I was tense as a violin string, afraid his fingers might explore further than my head and face.

Why didn't I tell Natalie about Hugo? I didn't deliberately deceive – or, as she thought, *betray* – her. In my head, I thought of my time with Hugo as my art life, my heart life. That almost became a kind of song in my head – *my art life/my heart life*. And it was separate from everything and everyone else. I didn't want to think of sharing Hugo with anyone. Not even Philip.

That week, the week when I didn't know if Mr Oliver was alive or dead, it was impossible to sit still for Hugo.

Hugo ended up throwing the charcoal across the caravan in exasperation. 'Impossible!' he howled. 'Impossible girl, sea nymph, whatever you are. You can't sit still. You're all jitters and twitches. What's the matter?' And he knelt in front of me, grabbed my hands in his and studied my face.

I pulled away. I wished I could just put my arms round his neck and sob. But I couldn't. I couldn't tell.

'Well, if you can't sit still, let's have some action,' said Hugo.

I didn't have the heart for paddling or throwing pebbles. Even sitting cross-legged and sticking my tongue out as Hugo suggested didn't make me laugh.

'Dance, then!' he shouted, spreading his arms as if the beach was a ballroom.

'Dance?' Immediately I felt incredibly stiff and awkward.

'You know how to dance, don't you? Everyone knows how to dance.'

'There's no music,' I protested. I was getting hotter and hotter with embarrassment. I knew I was flushing.

'I'll hum,' Hugo said.

So he hummed and clapped and almost in despair I gave in and danced. And then for all of five minutes I completely forgot myself. I danced for Hugo. For the summer. For the hope that everything would come right.

Hugo stopped humming and it all came back to me. Mr Oliver dead or dying because we'd frightened the life out of him.

'I need to get home,' I said.

'Ah, you're a poor troubled soul!' said Hugo, putting on a mock Irish accent. 'Come back when you've got rid of the twitches and jitters.'

Lal said much the same when she and Paul took me to see the flat they were hoping to buy.

'Are you on another planet?' was how she put it. I seemed to have grown nervous tics I couldn't stop – putting my hands in and out of my pockets, tapping one foot, rubbing my ear.

Paul had been home a week. I'd forgotten how tall, blond and handsome he was. I'd given up hope of Lal falling out of love with him. I kept coming upon the two of them – *the love birds*, as Mum called them – cuddling and kissing. I had to keep backing out of the room, saying, 'Sorry, sorry, sorry,' or tiptoeing away, trying to close the door ever so quietly behind me. It was embarrassing. And it made me feel lonely like it does when you know two people who are best friends and you haven't got one of your own. Of course, I had Natalie, and I still thought Natalie was more alive and exciting than anyone I'd ever met, but also moody, unpredictable, wild. *Passionate* was how I thought of Natalie, and no one else had as much passion as she had. Except possibly Hugo. Only his kind of passion was quiet and intense and just went in one direction – his painting. Neither Natalie nor Hugo were what you might call comfortable people. Not comfortable like Alice and Dottie had been. Not comfortable like Lal and Paul seemed when they were together.

'We'll have to have a spare bed here for you, Little Sis,' Paul said. He'd taken to calling me that. It got on my nerves. I knew he was trying to be nice to me and the more he tried, the nastier I got.

'Please yourself!' I said now.

'Why are you so horrid?' Lal asked. 'Are you going to scowl your way through the wedding?'

I wanted to say that 'horrid' was how I felt and that it was impossible to feel any other way if you thought you might possibly have murdered someone.

The only person I could really talk to was Natalie. And Natalie and I didn't agree.

'If Mr Oliver's dead,' Natalie said, 'it's just because he's old.' You could drop dead just like that if you were old, she claimed, and if that was what had happened, then GRBR – good riddance to bad rubbish – because it meant there was one less Left-Over Nazi in the world.

'We should celebrate,' said Natalie, but for once she didn't sound convincing, and though neither of us suggested going back to Mr Oliver's house to look, we just kept on talking and arguing about him.

'Dead, dead, dead!' Philip would chant whenever he heard the name Mr Oliver.

I began to get nightmares in which Mr Oliver was lying dead under his desk or had gone off to the unknown Headquarters to tell them about us. Sometimes I'd wake in the middle of the night imagining Nazis in jackboots hammering at the door. It was a relief to hear Dad's cough or Mum's slippers on the creaky step to the lavatory.

Natalie refused to be shaken. '*If* he is dead,' she said, 'someone else would have found him by now – a relative or someone.'

'I don't think he has any relatives,' I said.

Natalie shrugged. 'Well, someone,' she said. 'Because he'd start smelling. And if he isn't dead,' she went on, 'then it's a pity we didn't get the chance to interrogate him.'

'Interrogate him?'

'Get him to the air-raid shelter. Get him to give us a list of names. That's what you do.' Suddenly the conviction that I'd always admired in Natalie – that lack of doubt, lack of guilt – made me feel scared. It was so cold. So next to ruthless.

It struck me that interrogation had been in Natalie's mind all along. I pictured Mr Oliver kneeling on the floor of the shelter, Natalie shining a torch in his eyes to make him talk, and felt slightly sick. I'd no desire to interrogate Mr Oliver or anyone else.

It had been easy when our LONs just upped and offed like Sam Dingle and Maisie Lewis. Out of sight, out of mind. That's what Mum used to say when she didn't want to think about something. Only it didn't work at all with Mr Oliver. It was precisely *because* he was out of sight that I couldn't get him out of my mind.

And what if he did give us a list of names? It was a terrible thought. It meant we could be stalking LONs for years, long after Lal and Paul were married, long after I'd left school even, way, way into the future. Natalie's *Messages* book would get fatter and fatter with crossed-out names. Crossed-out people.

It had all gone wrong. The whole summer had gone wrong. Gone nasty. I saw myself sacrificing my entire life to routing out evil; days and nights spent interrogating people in the damp darkness of the air-raid shelter. I almost wished Mr Oliver *was* dead.

I nagged at Natalie. I wanted her with me. I wanted her worried, doubting, maybe even guilty. Maybe I just meant normal. How else could we be kindred spirits? In the end, my constant 'What if's over Mr Oliver, my constant jitters, drove Natalie to say, 'Well, *you* go. *You* go and look if you're that worried.'

'What? Go back to his house?'

'Where else? The cemetery?'

'I can't go on my own!' I said.

We'd walked to the end of the pier again. We did that sometimes as if remembering our first meeting, Natalie's dare. I was glad Hugo didn't seem to be about, though just a glimpse of the yellow caravan cheered me up. Philip had run off. To Hugo? I wondered.

Natalie sighed and stood up, dusting down her shorts, hitching her bag up on her shoulder. 'Well, maybe you don't really care,' she said. 'Maybe you're just not tough enough for this. Not serious. A poor little rich girl. I should have known better.' And she sauntered away.

I stayed where I was, my legs dangling over the end of the pier. I knew she was challenging me. And I knew I had to do it.

I had to go back to Mr Oliver's house.

The Caravan
Six a.m. on a beautiful morning

Dear Helena,
Please *tell Derek he doesn't need to worry. There will be plenty of paintings for the exhibition and I'll make sure he gets them in good time. The new ones will include the following portraits:*

Mrs Nancy Kipper, *the fish-cart woman.*

Ailsa and Fiona Kettle *(otherwise known as the old maids from the sweet shop – I've done them in their long white aprons).*

Sam Dingle, *the garage man.*

Hans Oliver. *He's the Hungarian refugee – a very solitary soul and it's been really hard work making friends with him and getting him to let me draw and paint him. Of course I could have talked to him about Auschwitz and about what happened to Ma, Pa and Jo. He would have had similar stories to tell. But it didn't feel right. Instead we talked about music. And that's because Hans was a violinist. I wangled a visit to his house and got him to play for me. He came alive! Anyway, the painting is far from finished, not least because he hasn't turned up in his usual haunts for days.*

And of course there'll be a number of paintings of Lizzie and Philip. I won't name them. I want titles like 'Boy Drawing' or 'Sleeping Child' or 'Girl Paddling'. All I've got of the Wild One is a quick sketch I dashed off while she shouted at me that I was a second-rate artist. Only Van Gogh would be good enough for her! I need something much more detailed and time is running out.

I'm worried about Philip. I think the boy would like to move in if he could, though as soon as he sees Lizzie coming he's off and away. I don't think it's Lizzie he's worried about. I think it's that sister of his. The Wild One. Also, although sometimes I draw some patterns for him and suggest he might like to colour them in, he still likes to scrub away at what I call his 'fiery pictures'.

'Is that my cooking fire?' I ask him. 'Because it's a bit big. My sausages would be burned to a cinder!'

He just laughs at that and carries on with the reds, oranges and yellows which are now almost worn to stubs. I shall have to buy him more.

Actually, it's not much use asking him anything because his answers don't make much sense. 'Where's your dad?' I asked him one day.

'Flown away,' he says, flapping his arms. 'Flown.'

He likes looking at the portraits. He stares at them with his thumb in his mouth and then comes out with odd comments that don't make any sense. So he looks at the portrait of Sam Dingle (he's the garage man) and he says, 'Man ran away.' Now what's that about? Has Sam gone away? Or is he about to go away? I've no idea. What really worried me was that he looked at the unfinished portrait of Hans Oliver, made a cross with his two forefingers and chanted, 'Dead! Dead! Dead!'

'Course he's not dead!' I said. 'Maybe you're thinking of one of those uncles of yours.' Really I was quite cross with him. I shooed him off home with a pat on the behind. Told him to come back tomorrow. He gave me a hug and went.

It's made me think that I'd better go and see Hans. Make sure he isn't dead!

Oh, I meant to say . . . please tell Derek that I really want to include some of my landscapes in the exhibition. Particularly the slightly surreal ones and the ones you call 'disturbed'. I want the whole range of my work. Not just the sunny stuff.

I'll start thinking about a date to bring up the first paintings. And yes, a list of people to invite to the preview.

Have faith. It will all happen.

Love as always,
Hugo

Natalie's Diary

Sunday

Dodgy Doug was back last night. Late. Him and Ma both drunk and rowing as usual. Why does she even let him in? He's the worst of them all. After midnight and he starts bashing at my door. Something about Ma being past it.

'You're next in line . . .' he says and he thinks this is so funny he falls down the stairs. Then I hear Ma shouting at him and the front door banging. And Mrs Nivens from next door calling Ma names and going on about bringing down the neighbourhood. Just in case, me and Philip shoved Philip's mattress against the door, then he came into my bed. Kicked and wriggled all night.

If Mr Oliver is dead I'm going to run away. Me and Philip. We could hitch to London. If I dress up I look much older. There's lorries that will stop. Lizzie thinks I don't care. I think Lizzie might break down and tell someone. Mr Artist, that's who she might tell. I think she's in love with him. I've got to watch her. What if she betrays me? What if she doesn't keep to the Vow?

NB to Self. No one stays with you for ever. No one. Get tough. Get used to it. One day you'll not need anyone. That's what to work towards. Being self sufficient. Needing no one. Not even Philip. One day. Aim at 17.

It's Mr Artist I've got to deal with. Artists are clever and deceitful. They make things up. Well, I'm cleverer than he is! So there, Mr Artist! You wait and see. I've seen you watching me! I've seen that look in your eyes, like the men who look at Ma. You think you're special just because you're good looking and you can paint a few pictures. Well, just you watch out, Mr Artist. I've got your number. You won't take Lizzie and Philip away. I can turn them against you, easy as that. Watch out, Mr Artist, that's what I say. Watch out!

What if Mr Oliver is dead like Philip says? Does Philip know? Does Philip just want him dead? I can't get any sense out of him just now. And he keeps coming home with new clothes – well, new old clothes that that artist has got for him. I don't say anything. Not yet, anyway.

Maybe I should go to Mr Oliver's house like Lizzie keeps suggesting. No. Bad idea. Someone might see us at the scene of the crime. If there is a scene of the crime which there isn't because all we were doing was getting rid of another LON.

NB to Self. Keep reminding yourself that that's what we were doing.

If we don't see Mr Oliver for . . . how long? Two weeks? Three? Then he has to be dead. Say GRBR. GRBR.

Another LON gone. Da will be pleased.

Chapter 13

Cockles and Mussels

I went the next morning. Early. It might have been safer at night but I didn't have the nerve. I set my alarm for five. The birds had just started up. Strips of darkness were peeling off the sky like old paint. One of Mum's old coats was hanging in the hall together with a hat. The coat was too big for me and the hat came down over my eyes but at least I felt hidden and there was a pocket for a torch. I should have oiled the bolts on the front door but I hadn't. I eased them back slowly, gritting my teeth at the squeaks. At least I managed not to let the garden gate bang, which it does if you allow it to fall shut behind you. Then I took a deep breath. I was out.

I don't think I've ever been out quite so early. Norton was still asleep. The streetlights switched themselves off as I walked down the road. Who told them to do it? Even though there was no one about, I kept my head down and walked quickly. I wished I hadn't picked Mum's old brown coat. It went down to my ankles. I looked either mad or criminal. Not that there was anyone watching. In one house there was a lighted bedroom window – either someone off to work very early or someone who couldn't sleep. The only other light came from a side ward of the cottage hospital. What if Mr Oliver was there? Rescued and given the kiss of life by a stranger and taken to the hospital. Just now, at 5.30 a.m., they could be pumping him with oxygen or whatever they do to people who are nearly dying. And if they saved him, would he tell about us? Not if he really *was* a LON. And if he wasn't . . . ?

By the time I reached the lane of Mr Oliver's house I was missing Natalie so much I could hear her voice in my head. All the things she'd said, only muddled up, out of order. *Good riddance to bad rubbish. We should celebrate! We should celebrate! Interrogate him! Get a list of names!*

The curtains at the front of the house were still drawn. A tongue of envelopes stuck out of the letter box. How long had they been there? I looked up at the top front window. The curtains weren't drawn there, but there'd be a bedroom at the back, wouldn't there? He could be tucked up asleep. Did he wear his funny hat in bed? Maybe with a nightshirt like an old Wee Willie Winkie? There was no way out of it – I'd have to go round the back of the house. I'd have to break in. My heart began pounding so hard that I had to bend over double and take deep breaths.

I tried to get up my nerve by having an imaginary conversation with Natalie. I'd tell her what I'd done. She'd be impressed. I'd see the admiration in her eyes. She'd never call me a poor little rich girl again. Then I pushed round the bushes at the back of Mr Oliver's house. They were so rough and overgrown – one was holly – that Mr Oliver must have given up using his back door. Twigs and leaves stuck to my awkward coat. I wished I could dump it only Mum would miss it. There was one of those corrugated glass panels in the back door that stop you seeing through; in any case, it was too dirty. I could just about see in the kitchen window. There was a pan on the cooker and dishes in the sink. How long had they been there?

Was this Mr Oliver's last supper? There were the remains of a loaf of bread on the kitchen table. It looked old but not mouldy. How long did bread last? Perhaps I could just give up now. Persuade Natalie and Philip to come with me.

I tried the back door and discovered I didn't need to break in. It wasn't locked. Of course it wasn't locked! All those bushes were lock enough. No one would bother to push past them. I took off my shoes and went in.

The first thing I heard was music. I stood and listened. I'd been so scared that Mr Oliver was dead that it never occurred to me to be scared that he was alive! What might he do if he heard an intruder? He might come at me with a knife or possibly a gun – surely every LON, if he *was* a LON, would have a gun? And if he didn't attack me, if he *wasn't* a LON, he'd call the police. Did he have a phone, and where was it? What did burglars do? Did they cut the line? I should have brought scissors.

I picked up the bread knife instead and crept into the hall. The music was coming from upstairs. It sounded like a radio because after a moment or two the music stopped and there was the voice of someone speaking. Then back to the music. I remembered that when we'd looked through the window into the front room we'd seen a radio. Had he taken it to bed with him? Was he lying there awake and waiting for me, the music just a decoy? Or was he dead in his bed, the radio left on? And should I check the front room? The shelf of books Natalie had said were German? His desk? Should I look? If Mr Oliver was the leader of a cell of Left-Over Nazis – as Natalie thought – there could be evidence. Evidence of a major LON plot. What a triumph if I took *that* back to Natalie! Even if it was the sort of triumph I badly didn't want.

Afterwards, I told myself. *I'll look afterwards. When I've found out if he's alive or dead.* I crept up the stairs. Several of them creaked. Each time I froze on one leg and waited. I followed the music to the back bedroom.

The door was open. At first all I saw was the small figure of Mr Oliver in bed, his head looking all bare and small without his hat. He had an old patchwork quilt pulled up round his shoulders and the radio on a table beside him.

Only when I pushed the door further open – just to make sure he was breathing – did I see him: Hugo. Hugo slumped asleep in a chair, a blanket round his shoulders, a sketchbook fallen on the floor beside him.

I fled.

I'm not sure how I got myself home. I hardly noticed the holly bush dragging at my hands, my hair, Mum's coat. I think I probably left Mr Oliver's back door wide open in my hurry to get out of there.

Such a relief! Mr Oliver was alive! I could have danced down the street singing that song about cockles and mussels being *alive, alive-o* if it wasn't for the big coat weighing me down. From relief I plunged into despair. Hugo! Hugo was Mr Oliver's friend! If Hugo discovered what Natalie and I had been doing, he'd never want to see or speak to me again. And then what? I'd be cut off from happiness like Mum was cut off from all her aunts and uncles and cousins. My life would be over.

I wanted to go straight to Natalie's and tell her the news but it wasn't even seven o'clock yet and anyway, I needed to get home before Mum found me missing. I just about made it. I heard Dad's morning cough and Mum padding down to the bathroom in her flapping slippers as I dumped the coat and hat, slipped off my shoes in the hall, ran upstairs and slid into bed, not bothering to take anything else off, just pulling the blankets and eiderdown up to my neck. With my ear pressed into the pillow I could hear my heart knocking like it wanted to get out. It calmed down a little when I heard Mum going downstairs and Dad's cough moving into his dressing room. I knew exactly what he did in there – sat on his wicker chair in his striped towelling dressing gown, legs splayed open, specs off, smoking and pondering, pondering and smoking, like he did for hours every morning. When I was little I used to think he was like Jacob struggling with an angel – until Mum told me he was just thinking about business. I guessed now that he was probably thinking about the wedding and how to let everyone know that we had enough money for a really grand one. I didn't want to think about that. I felt as if I was the one struggling with two angels, one good, one bad, both of them mine.

After a while spent pretending to be half asleep, I got up and sauntered downstairs as if it was any ordinary morning. Lal was just about to go to work, all fresh and pretty in her gingham summer dress. She'd be going to meet Paul after work.

'Ye gods,' she said, 'you look like something the cat's brought in!'

'And you're Miss Perfect,' I said.

'I just can't help being wonderful and beautiful,' Lal said, ruffling my already ruffled hair. Then she was off, slamming the door behind her, calling, 'Bye,' as she went. I heard her heels clicking down the path as if she was tapping out *happiness* with her feet.

I ate a piece of toast as fast as I could and said I was off to the beach. Dad was totally occupied with his bacon and drippy fried egg. The post had arrived. Mum was flicking through the letters to see if there were any replies to the wedding invitations yet. I was out of the house before either of them had time to really notice.

It was still very early to arrive at Natalie's and even standing on the doorstep I could hear a terrible racket going on inside – Mrs Rafferty shouting and Philip crying. Before I had time to knock, a man burst out of the front door half dressed. Mrs Rafferty came out behind him and flung his jacket at him. He slouched off down the road. I thought Natalie's uncles were a strange and unpleasant lot. Maybe it was better not to know your uncles. Better to be cut off.

'Oh, it's you,' said Mrs Rafferty. 'Have you any idea what time it is? Morning hasn't quite happened according to my watch.'

I don't think Mrs Rafferty was wearing a watch but before I could answer Natalie appeared. She looked pale and there was a great bruise on the top of her arm. She covered it over with her hand and scowled at me. 'Wait there!' she said.

I waited, remembering how fascinated I'd been on that first visit to Natalie's house. I'd thought her house was exciting, that you could do anything you liked and no one bossed you, that it wasn't dull like my house with Mum and Dad settled in front of the television and real life kept out by fitted carpets and velvet curtains and money.

This morning I thought that maybe I'd got it all wrong. I'd seen just what I wanted to see, not how it really was. How it really was, was Natalie coming out of the house pulling on a jersey to hide the bruise and dragging Philip, his face a smear of tears and whatever he last ate, with her.

'The air-raid shelter,' she said. Mrs Rafferty shouted after us, but Natalie ignored her. We didn't go inside the shelter. Neither of us said we couldn't face the darkness but I think that's how it was. I knew by the set of her face not to mention the uncles. So we just leaned our backs against the rough concrete of the shelter, as if this time it was sheltering us. We just sat there for a minute without saying anything. Then Natalie produced a half-bar of chocolate from the pocket of her shorts, gave it to Philip and said, 'Well?'

'He's alive,' I said. 'Mr Oliver's alive!'

'So you really went there?' A look that was the nearest to admiration I'd ever seen her give flashed across Natalie's face before she doused it.

'Yes. He was in bed—'

'Not dying?'

'Not dying, not dying, not dying!' chanted Philip cheerfully.

Was Natalie pleased? I couldn't tell.

'No,' I said. 'Not well, but not dying – no, definitely not dying because there was someone with him—'

Natalie looked alarmed. 'Someone *with* him? Who?'

I couldn't help but smile. It was the moment I'd been waiting for. This was when I could tell her that as far as Mr Oliver was concerned, we'd got it wrong. Mr Oliver couldn't possibly be a LON and if we'd got *that* wrong maybe we'd got the whole thing wrong. I wanted a way out, a way out of the quest, the Vow. I wanted my life back, summer back, even ordinary, peacefully dull Norton back. I wanted all that and I still wanted Natalie as my kindred spirit.

'Who was with him? Who?' Natalie asked again.

'Hugo,' I said. Just saying his name pleased me. 'Hugo was with him.'

'Hugo? The artist in the caravan?' Natalie's eyes had turned as dark as if she'd poured ink into them. I should have been warned.

'Philip likes y-y-yellow caravan,' said Philip. He'd wriggled himself into the crook of Natalie's arm.

'Shut up,' said Natalie.

'I think he must have stayed with Mr Oliver all night,' I said. 'He was sitting in a chair beside the bed with a blanket round him and his sketchbook, and he'd fallen asleep too, so you see if Hugo was with him, Mr Oliver *can't* be a LON!'

I heard myself sounding like a preacher in church – certain of what I believed. It was my turn to be free of doubt. My turn to have conviction.

Natalie said nothing and I'd never known a louder silence. She just looked at me as if she was seeing a stranger. Although the sun was getting up now and toasting the side of the shelter, I felt suddenly cold. Chilled. As if I'd caught a chill of the heart.

'L-l-l-like to live in a yellow caravan,' said Philip.

'Shut up!' said Natalie. And turning to me, speaking in a voice just a little above a whisper, 'Now, is that so?'

Natalie's Diary

Very late

Mr Oliver and Mr Artist – Hugo's his name – they're a team! It's worse than a cell of LONs. They're recruiting. Getting children. Once they get the children, they've got a way to the parents. That's why the artist paints children.

Mr Artist, he's won Lizzie over. She danced for him! I saw her. Philip and me hid behind the sea wall, watching. Philip didn't want to but I made him. How could she? How could she do it? As if she was his dancing bear on a chain.

He was shouting instructions at her while he pretended to draw. Well, he was drawing but I know that's only a front. I've worked it out. He had her doing just what he wanted. Paddle! Throw pebbles! Stick your tongue out. Anything! And she'd do it. He's brain-washed her.

'You know how to dance, don't you?' he says. 'Everyone knows how to dance.'

And I'm behind the wall praying she'll say no, say she doesn't know how to dance. She won't dance. She won't do what he says just like Ma does what all the men tell her. I have to pinch Philip to keep him quiet.

I can just about hear Lizzie. 'There's no music,' she says.

'I'll hum,' he says. And that's what he does and you couldn't call it singing, not by any stretch of the imagination, but he hums and claps and even Philip's feet begin to jig until I slap him.

And Lizzie dances. It brings the tears to my eyes, she looks so lovely, my Lizzie, like she's forgetting everything when she dances. When she stops and goes away, I stop thinking how lovely she is and I feel really mad, and I grab Philip by the hand and we come out from behind the wall and down we go onto the beach, walking really slowly and all the way I'm fixing that Mr Artist with a look. I don't take my eyes off him. I'm telling him with my eyes that I know.

Only he doesn't look guilty or shamed or anything. He just stares right back at me, and then he shouts, '*Hold it! Hold that pose!*' That was such a shock that I did. I could see Mr Artist turn a page of his sketchbook and start drawing me. His hand going like crazy over the paper. Once I knew what he was doing, I gave him two fingers.

'You're not even second rate!' I shouted.

He just laughed and kept on drawing. People can steal your soul when they take your picture or draw you. I've read about it.

Next thing though, Philip's pulled away from me and he's running to the artist, his feet kicking up sand and what does Mr Artist do? He puts down his sketchbook and swoops Philip up and swings him round and round. It's like he's welcoming him home.

So I'm screeching at him then. Screeching at both of them, but mainly at Philip and Philip's just not coming and not coming. He goes into the caravan and Mr Artist just shrugs as if none of this is his fault and the only thing I can do if I'm not to look a total idiot is stalk off. So I do. And I just let the tears run down my face without wiping them because I don't want him to guess I'm crying.

I've got to have a plan. He must have done something to Philip. Philip's Seeing has gone all wrong. Usually he picks up exactly what I'm thinking. It's about the only thing Ma ever got right, years ago when we were in London and Philip was only – what? Four? Five? 'You two,' Ma said, 'you've got some kind of telepathy going. It's creepy! Pack it in!' And Philip and I just fell about laughing. It must have been soon after that that Philip began his Seeing. And I've been – what d'you call those stage people who help when an actor forgets his lines? – a Prompt. That's what I've been. Or that's what I thought I've been. Just stroking his head, or his back between his shoulder blades when we were watching the garage man. Or Mr Oliver. But maybe I've not been. A Prompt, that is. And maybe he's sort of left me. The telepathy's gone.

NB to Self. Get the drawing.

Chapter 14

A Choice

I didn't want to choose. I didn't want it to be Natalie *or* Hugo. Hugo *or* Natalie. I kept pushing away the thought that I might have to – choose, that is. It was mid August. We were in the middle of a heat wave. It was so hot and close you felt there was a storm coming, one of those freaky summer storms that brings out the lifeboat in the middle of the night or has the Council padding the sea wall with sandbags in a mostly hopeless attempt to stop the sea leaping the wall and rushing for the houses.

Natalie's mood matched the weather. Brooding. Stormy. Sort of silently stormy which somehow was more scary than if she'd completely lost her temper. She knew I'd been letting Hugo draw me. Somehow or other she'd seen me dancing for him!

'You're just soppy about him,' she'd say, always with a kind of sneer that made me squirm. 'He'll be away soon. He'll forget all about you.'

'He'll have the drawings,' I said. I wasn't going to tell her about my dream. My dream that the summer I turned sixteen Hugo would come for me and we'd go off together. We'd live happily ever after in the yellow caravan (or wherever Hugo lived in the winter) and I'd be his muse. Did artists marry their muses? I wasn't too sure. Well, that was the dream. Actually, Philip got in the way of the dream. Philip had done what I didn't quite have the courage to do yet. He'd chosen. Chosen Hugo. I think he'd been visiting Hugo secretly for weeks. I guessed this not only because I'd once seen him leaving the caravan but because lately I kept finding drawings he'd done. Not really drawings. Just pages of wax crayoning, every page the same. Flames of red, orange, yellow, like Philip wanted to set everything on fire. I thought I might feel that way if I lived in his house.

That afternoon when Natalie found me dancing for Hugo, that had somehow been the moment when Philip made his choice, pulling away from Natalie and running into Hugo's arms. It had stabbed at my heart seeing that. The look on Philip's face. Hugo's wide open arms. They loved each other and it was stupid being jealous of an eight-year-old boy, but somehow I was.

Without Philip, there was something lost about Natalie. I'd hardly ever seen her without Philip hanging onto her hand, her sleeve, her leg. It was as if she'd lost a part of herself. Until those last weeks of the summer holidays, Philip had never gone anywhere without Natalie. Now, almost as soon as he was awake, he was off on his own, heading for Hugo's caravan. If Hugo was out, Philip would sit on the caravan step, his eyes half closed, rocking and crooning to himself, his arms around his knees. I'd seen him there myself one morning when I was still trying to get up the nerve to go back to the caravan.

It took me days after I'd found Mr Oliver still alive, and Hugo with him, to brave a visit. I wished I could be like Philip, sure of a welcome. But I wasn't. Had Mr Oliver told Hugo about Natalie and me and all our hounding and following? If he had, I doubted Hugo would ever speak to me again. Probably his smile, which warmed the very heart of me, would be switched off for ever. He'd turn his back. That's what he'd do. Turn his back.

Yet somehow I couldn't keep away. I had to risk it. Something like a magnet drew me back – to the cheer of the yellow caravan, to the looking and painting, to Hugo's life on the beach. To Hugo. Hugo, who at the end of the summer would pack up his caravan and leave Norton for the winter. Come winter, both Hugo and Lal would be gone.

I almost collapsed with relief when Hugo greeted me with, 'So where have you been hiding yourself? Sea nymphs aren't allowed to wander off like that. Has nobody told you?'

And it was more easy than I could ever have hoped to ask him about Mr Oliver, because Hugo had a sketch of him pinned up on the easel.

'What d'you think of it?' he asked.

'It's like,' I said. 'Very like. Do you know him well?' I half expected Hugo to notice the tremble in my voice, but he didn't. Instead he started telling me about how he'd met Mr Oliver – Hans, as he called him – sitting in the shelter with his fish and his newspaper and how they'd got friendly, though it hadn't been easy and Hans didn't have very good English, but eventually he'd agreed to Hugo drawing him.

'I'm going to miss him,' Hugo said.

'Miss him?' For an awful moment I thought that maybe Mr Oliver *had* died after all.

'His sisters have been trying to persuade him to come and live with them for years,' said Hugo. 'He gave in after he had that bout of flu. It really laid him low. So now the sisters have got their way. Taken him off to Kent to look after him. Probably boss him about – they looked like that kind of sister.'

It was obvious that Mr Oliver *hadn't* told Hugo about Natalie and me – either because he'd been too poorly to do so or because he didn't have time before the sisters arrived. And it had been flu, not us following him and taunting him, that had laid him low in his bed. The relief of it went through me like a blood transfusion into a very poorly person.

'Poor old Hans,' Hugo continued. 'He had such a raging temperature I thought he was delirious. Going on about people being after him. I stayed with him in case he needed to go to hospital, and also because he was frightened of being alone. Maybe that goes back to him being a refugee.'

'A refugee?'

'Didn't you know? Well, I suppose there's no reason you should. A Jewish refugee. He escaped from Hungary during the war. He was a violinist in Hungary, but he never played again. Sad!'

I tried to tell Natalie about Mr Oliver being a Jewish refugee and playing the violin and how Hugo had made friends with him and drawn pictures of him like he'd done of Mrs Kipper, the fish-cart woman, and the old maids in the sweet shop, who wore long white aprons, and the man we called 'the baby man' because he loved looking in prams. People liked talking to Hugo because, even if he came every summer, he wasn't permanent, he was just passing through. You could tell him a secret and he'd take it away with him. You felt he'd keep it safe. And Hugo liked odd characters. Maybe I was one of them.

But Natalie only looked at me as if I was stupid. 'Love's blind!' she said with a roll of her eyes.

It was on the tip of my tongue to say, *And maybe hate is too.* But I didn't. We'd walked to the end of the pier again. It was something we still liked to do. Something that still kept us together, walking out there where no one else dared, sitting at the very edge of the sea, arms about each other. We were together as we'd been at the beginning of the summer, only now there was no Philip waiting for us.

'Aren't you pleased that Philip's not tagging along with you all the time?' I tried.

'I don't want that artist messing with Philip,' Natalie said. 'He probably likes all little boys.'

She said it as if there was something wrong with liking little boys that I didn't know about. I couldn't help but defend Hugo.

'Hugo's an OK person,' I said stoutly. 'He just likes Philip.'

'No one likes Philip,' said Natalie. 'Who would? Funny leg, funny face, a bit daft.'

'Well, *you* do,' I said. I was asking myself if I liked Philip, and somehow liking didn't come into it. Mostly I thought him a sad, spooky little boy who got in the way and was always wanting something. Lately I'd got jealous of the way Hugo was prepared to spend so much time with him. And was Philip really a Seer as Natalie claimed he was? He'd got it very wrong about Mr Oliver. What if he'd been wrong about Sam Dingle and Maisie Lewis? What if what he'd seen inside these people hadn't been a swastika (as Natalie said it was) but something else?

'Philip's my brother,' Natalie said. She looked at me with that fierce, defiant look she had. A look of someone permanently threatened. One of her sandals dangled from her toe as if she could just let it fall and drop and wouldn't care. 'He's my brother,' she repeated, 'and I love him more than anyone.'

'Only natural,' I said nervously. There was something in her voice that scared me. 'I bet he loves you more than anyone,' I said.

'Not since he's taken to your Mr Artist,' Natalie said.

'Hugo's not mine,' I said weakly. (If only!)

'He's distracting him,' Natalie said. 'Philip's forgetting about the LONs. Maybe you are too?' Her eyes, when she turned to look at me, seemed to look right through to my soul.

'No. No, of course not!' I said, because even then, even when I had some kind of inkling that this was all going wrong, that Natalie had something terrible in mind, I still couldn't quite let her go. Couldn't give up on her the way you can't give up an idea that was once very lovely, that perhaps still could be.

'Kindred spirits,' I said, but I knew I didn't believe in it any more. And I think Natalie knew too.

'Philip will get fed up with Hugo,' I said. 'He'll come back to us. To you.'

Even as I said it, I thought it was a lie.

The Caravan
2 a.m. and sleepless

Dear Helena,
You're right, of course. I've got too involved. And yes, I know that nothing and no one can bring Jo back and that Philip's got a life and a family of his own, and I could do more harm than good if the boy gets too fond . . . et cetera, et cetera. I do know all that, Helena, I really do. But what you don't understand, because you're not here, you haven't met him, is that no one really looks after the child. And I'm afraid I just lost my temper when I realized he couldn't see through those specs shoved on his nose. The world must be a total blur to the child.

D'you remember those debates we used to have about which would be worse, to be blind or deaf, and you chose deaf because you couldn't bear to be without music and I chose blind because I couldn't bear not to see?

I discovered Philip couldn't see when I sent him to buy ice cream and he couldn't even see the ice-cream van! So when that sister of his came to collect him – she's the Wild One, and believe you me, she's beginning to make me a bit wild – that's when I lost my temper. I took the specs and waved them under her nose.

'Where did these come from?' I asked her. 'D'you know he can't see?'

Then Philip himself pipes up with, 'Ma found them!'

Found them! They could be anybody's specs. You could really damage your eyes using glasses with the wrong lenses in them. I gave the Wild One a demonstration. Lizzie was here too so I made her stand some distance away, and then I asked Philip to tell us what she was wearing on her head. (Nothing, was the answer.) Philip tried a hat, a ribbon, a slide, a flower. When none of them was right, he took off the specs, rubbed his eyes and said it was all 'a bit watery'.

The Wild One was just standing there, hands on hips, looking at me with that mocking look she's got. She must have developed it by dipping it in poison or something.

'Why don't you just mind your own business?' she said. Said? More like she spat.

'Because,' I said, 'your brother's going around half blind! He needs an optician. He needs proper specs.'

OK, so I shouldn't have shouted. I shouldn't have lost my temper. Next thing, she's grabbed hold of Philip and she's screeching at me and dragging him away.

I'm not entirely sure what she was screeching but it sounded like, 'He can see things you can't.' What could she mean? Was Philip haunted or something? Was it to do with the bastard uncles? Whatever it was, it gave me the creeps. I'd been really relieved to find that Philip's notion about Hans Oliver being dead wasn't true. I'd been to see him and found him very poorly, but very alive. I'd decided that Philip's head was full of all sorts of daft notions. But now there was this crazy sister of his claiming he can see things.

Anyway, there was no way I could ask her while she was dragging him away shouting, 'He doesn't need you! He doesn't need you!' And I'm thinking, He damn well does. He does! He does! *And Philip's dragging his feet, looking over his shoulder and sobbing, and Lizzie's just standing there as if she's in shock. I could tell she couldn't decide whether to stay or go, so I sent her off. I needed time to cool down.*

Ah! Never mind perspective in art – maybe I need a little in life. I can see you nodding your head and telling me that's what I was always a bit short of. Well, perhaps a little distance from the trio I seem to have spent most of the summer with will be a good thing. I plan to bring some of the paintings up for Derek in a couple of weeks' time – I know he's getting anxious. I'll stay over, and you and I will do grown-up things. A meal at Luigi's? Maybe a film? What d'you say?

Love as always,
Hugo

Chapter 15

Specs

Hugo took Philip to the optician and got him new specs. He'd been furious when he found that Philip couldn't see properly through his old specs and this was the result. A new pair that had little wire rims, fitted neatly round his ears and had Philip's proper sight in them.

Philip was delighted. Natalie wasn't just angry. She was maddened. It sounds kind of crazy, but in a way Natalie thought of Philip's eyes as hers. Or rather, of what he could and couldn't see as in her control. And now Hugo – Mr Artist, as she kept calling him with that sneer in her voice – was taking Philip over. Or that's how she saw it.

She snatched the specs from Philip's nose and would have smashed them if Philip hadn't burst into tears and if I hadn't grabbed them from her. We were in the air-raid shelter. Natalie had called a meeting. It was our last time there.

'It's a bribe,' she said. 'Can't you both see that? It's just a bribe.'

'What's a b-b-bribe?' Philip asked. 'I can see p-p-proper.'

'Something you're given that puts you in the other person's power,' said Natalie. 'And in your case, something that *stops* you seeing proper.'

I knew she meant Philip's other kind of Seeing.

'Hugo gives me b-b-butties,' Philip said. 'And crayons. I's going now. He'll be waiting.'

We watched him half skipping, half running over the sand hills towards the beach and the caravan. I thought he looked happy.

'See!' said Natalie. 'See what I mean?'

'No,' I said. 'I don't.'

'Hugo's got him in his power,' she told me. 'Philip's our eyes, remember. We need him to do the Seeing.'

'Maybe he just needs a bit of a rest,' I tried. 'Maybe the Seeing hurts him. He's only eight.'

For myself, I didn't want Philip to do any more Seeing. I didn't want another Mr Oliver. Yet somehow I couldn't rid my mind of those Left-Over Nazis. The fear of them came back to me at night when the house was silent or when I could hear the lifeboat going out with its maroon crying like the air-raid sirens used to do. It was still easy for Natalie to draw me back into her fears. Sometimes I thought it was the air-raid shelter itself that did it, as if the fear people must have felt in there when the bombs were falling still hung in the air, in the dank darkness of the place. I thought of the way Mum insisted on having very bright lights all over the house as if we weren't allowed any shadows. As if the war was a terrible black shadow and she was banishing it. And I thought of Hugo, looking towards the sea and saying he was trying to catch the light. Then I thought of Natalie, soon after I'd met her, asking how evil could just stop. And I thought you couldn't banish shadows and you couldn't catch the light without there being shadows. It seemed odd, but I thought that feelings went on as if every feeling had a kind of life of its own that went out into the world. You sent out your feelings and they kind of went to work despite you.

All this went round and round in my head. The Vow we'd made at the beginning of the summer. How we'd sworn to be kindred spirits. How good that had made me feel, as if I'd found something that would last for ever. And now I just wanted out and didn't know how to get out. If only it was as simple as just walking out of the air-raid shelter. And all the time I was struggling with ways to break the Vow, break the friendship, Natalie had plans of her own.

It began with a kind of tug-of-love over Philip. If he could, Philip would have left home and moved in with Hugo. Unless Natalie made a major fuss he was off there first thing in the morning, and it was Hugo who sent him, reluctantly, home. Philip slowly began moving his few possessions into the caravan like a bird making a nest. First his blankie. Then a box of old toys. Then his worn-to-the-stick toothbrush, his Mickey Mouse alarm clock that didn't work, a spare, if equally tatty, jersey. Hugo cleared a small shelf and part of a cupboard for what he called 'Philip's kit'. Some days I'd see the pair of them walking along the shoreline, both barefoot, Philip talking away to himself as he often did, or Hugo pointing at something that made Philip laugh. They collected driftwood together for the campfires Hugo made. They cooked sausages in an old black pan and held slices of bread over the fire on long forks.

Of course I was jealous! Hugo never told Philip to go away because he was busy, never got impatient with him as he did with me. Hugo filled sketchbook after sketchbook with drawings of Philip. He never got him to dance or pose. He just sketched him doing whatever he was doing. Philip paid no attention. Perhaps that's what Hugo liked – Philip just being Philip.

'He acts like he's Hugo's puppy!' Natalie said bitterly. It was true, in a way. When Hugo was working, Philip was happy to curl up on the bunk bed with some paper and wax crayons. Hugo taught him how to make tea on the little calor gas stove he kept in the caravan and – to Philip's obvious delight – got him to look after the biscuit tin. 'I've to make sure it's always half full,' Philip said, really pleased with himself. Apart from the specs, Hugo bought him new T-shirts and shorts from the second-hand shop. He made the Mickey Mouse alarm clock work again. He fed him.

'He'll go at the end of the summer,' Natalie warned Philip. She hadn't given up. She still thought she'd win Philip back. 'Then what'll you do?'

'Go with him,' Philip said stoutly.

'Don't you go thinking he'll want you,' said Natalie, 'because he won't.' That only made Philip cry and run back to the caravan. He began to take more things round as if he wanted to be ready for the day Hugo left. Not that he had much to take.

Then, strangely, as if fate had got out its weighing scales, as Philip took things to the caravan, other things – Hugo's things – began to go missing. Sketchbooks, canvases. One day in late August I found Hugo and Philip apparently in the middle of some kind of late spring cleaning. Everything was in a mess, paint tubes and drawing pads scattered about the place.

'I'm sorting the b-b-brushes,' Philip said, holding up a big jug and a handful of tufty brushes.

'Someone's been in,' said Hugo, handing Philip three more brushes and running his hand through his hair until it too was tufty. 'I don't know what's been taken. Who'd want to take anything?'

I felt as if something as heavy as an anchor had dropped down inside me. Who but Natalie? And as if she just happened to be passing, Natalie herself appeared.

Only Natalie as I'd never seen her before. She was wearing some kind of sarong she'd made, and she'd obviously borrowed her mother's make-up – mascara in particular, because her eyelashes were weighted with the stuff.

'Having fun, are we?' she called, and perched herself on the sea wall, crossing her legs like I'd seen models do in magazines.

She's come to preen, I thought, because she batted her eyelashes at Hugo and then smiled sweetly at me as if I was meant to know what she was up to, as if she could depend on me to be her ally, as if to remind me of the Vow. Hugo didn't seem to notice the eyelashes.

'I've been burgled,' he said. 'And the Lord knows why.'

'Perhaps he does,' said Natalie. 'The Lord. Know why, I mean.' She uncrossed and re-crossed her legs.

Hugo glared at her.

'I only meant He works in mysterious ways, or so they say,' she said lightly. 'Much taken?'

Just from that innocent enquiry I felt sure she'd done it. But why? What was the point? Stealing things from Hugo wasn't going to win Philip back. Maybe she was just hoping to make life in the caravan so unbearable for Hugo that he'd leave. And soon.

'Papers. Notes. Sketches. Two – no, three – small paintings,' said Hugo.

Natalie rearranged herself on the wall, hitching her sarong up a little. Was it just in the last two months that she'd grown breasts you really noticed?

'Tragic!' mocked Natalie. 'Works of genius lost to the world.' Another hitch of the sarong. I wondered if she learned all this from her mother. She put her hand to her hair and leaned back against the wall. Lazily.

Hugo grabbed a piece of paper and a stick of charcoal. He drew. Quickly, fiercely. I watched the charcoal mocking her as she'd mocked him. Hugo made a caricature of her, catching the sneer on her face, making the wildness of her hair look like a bird's nest, giving her bony shoulders like knives. The whole sketch made her look like an absurd bird of prey, a cross between girl and eagle. He flung the drawing at her.

'Very funny, Mr Second-rate Artist,' Natalie said, standing up. 'Come on, Philip, we're going.'

There was a long silence. Philip, on the edge of tears, chewed his lower lip.

Hugo sighed. 'Come on, old fellow. Better go with your sister,' he said, holding up his arms to lift Philip down from the bunk bed.

Natalie was already walking away. 'Philip! Hurry up!' she yelled.

But Philip had wriggled back into a corner of the bunk bed. 'Not coming!' he yelled back. 'Not coming! Not coming! Not coming!'

Natalie stopped and looked back. The look on her face was one I'd never seen before. She looked as if all her bravado had been taken away. Part of me – the part that still ached with kindred-spirit love – felt I should run after her, put my arm round her, leave Hugo and Philip behind. But I didn't. Like Philip, I'd made my choice. Perhaps you never make a choice with your head, only with your heart. At that moment I was furious with Natalie and sorry for Hugo. I stayed put.

Natalie's loss of bravado was brief. Within seconds she was tossing her hair, hands on hips, shouting, 'Do what you like, then. See if I care!' Stalking, strutting away.

Hugo burst out laughing. It was the last reaction I expected. The last reaction Natalie expected. A fatal reaction.

'Some girl!' Hugo said. 'I'm going to paint her if it's the last thing I do.'

Natalie's Diary

What day?

He'll laugh on the other side of his face. He's the real one. Not Sam Dingle. Not Maisie Lewis. Not Mr Oliver. They were like understudies. But he's like the Commandant. Of course they chose someone handsome. Someone who comes into the village. Watches. Now it's me who does the watching.

I need to act fast. I know the signs. We won't be here long now. Ma's getting restless. It's always the same. The neighbours getting nasty and Ma fighting back for a time. *Giving as good as I get*, she calls it. Then she gets tired. Weepy. Drunk. Weeks of rent owing. Then we're off.

Shall I tell Lizzie? Once, on the pier, Lizzie said, *Kindred spirits to the end of the world!* And I said, *To the end of time!* The sea was listening. The sea will always know.

I've only taken what's mine by rights. Drawings of Philip. There were some of Mr Oliver I didn't mean to take but they were mixed in.

I'll let him paint me. He'll think I've come round. He'll think I'm vain. He'll think I'm a walkover like Lizzie, like Philip – only Philip's too little to know any better. I'll be able to work everything out. How to destroy it all. I'll be a spy of a spy!

I whisper to Philip when he's asleep. I whisper, *He's a Left-Over Nazi. The artist's a Left-Over Nazi.*

But Philip won't dream it. He just won't dream it.

Note to Self. Rely on own dreams.

The Caravan
Supper time

Dear Helena,
A quick note. I'm going to bring the first batch of paintings up for Derek. Someone's been getting into the caravan and stealing stuff. In all the years I've been coming here that's never happened before. A sign of the times d'you think? Anyway, I don't want to risk losing anything else. I'll bring one batch this month and the rest before the end of September.

Oh, and I'm going to bring Philip. Please *don't give me a row. The boy's never had a holiday in his life. Seeing London, a couple of nights away from home – meeting you, Helena dear – will be an enormous adventure for him. He's madly excited already. Anyway, it's too late to tick me off. It's a done deal. I've got his mother's permission. My impression was that she was only too glad to get rid of him – the Freak, as she calls him – for a couple of days. I know you'll love him, Helena, so I'm almost sure you'll forgive me.*

Aside from all that – the important thing is that I've captured the Wild One! Well, not literally, of course. I mean in paint. It's taken all summer but I've finally got my trio. Lizzie, Philip and the Wild One – her name's Natalie, by the way. I'm not entirely sure why she agreed to sit for me. Maybe to win favour with Philip. Or perhaps there's some rivalry going on between her and Lizzie. Anyway, they don't seem so glued together as they did at the beginning of the summer. I wonder if they're growing up and growing apart?

Lizzie's still in short socks with a slide in her hair, while Natalie turned up for the sitting in a slinky dress and wearing scarlet lipstick. All very dramatic. She's got the most wonderful mop of hair. Of matching wildness you might say. She obviously had notions about being an artist's model and I have to admit that she's a natural.

Or would be if she could sit still for five minutes. Her eyes were everywhere. If eyes can ransack a place, that's what she was doing in the caravan. And you've never seen such anger in a young girl's eyes! That's what I'm going to call her portrait – 'Angry Girl' – it might well be the major one of the exhibition. We'll see.

Overall, the paintings I've done this summer surprise me. I'm pleased. It means that something just a little beyond myself has got in. Something from the subconscious, I suppose. And I've come to realize that I probably chose to paint children as a way of getting over my guilt about Jo. The guilt that I survived and he didn't. That I could have grabbed his hand and pulled him into the cupboard with us. But I didn't. I've painted living children as a way of keeping Jo alive. Maybe guilt will never entirely leave me and maybe that's a good thing, because if it did, I'd have lost even the memory of him.

The other surprise is that when I stand back and look at my trio, my trio as I've painted them, what I see is three children – three post-war *children, I think – who, although they're too young to remember the war, have somehow been blighted by it. It's almost as if they were born with the knowledge of war in their genes like a terrible inheritance. Was the horror of the concentration camps in the very air they breathed? Did they see pictures? Hear stories? I don't know. It's as if the memory of war has wounded them. Hurt their hearts, their minds. Their spirits.*

It's in those eyes of Lizzie's. Really ancient eyes she's got. And in the whole defiant, crazy look of the Wild One. And Philip? A lost soul if ever there was one, with a head full of nutty notions. But this reminds me – you'll be relieved to hear that he's stopped doing all those pictures of fires. That had me so worried I had to keep hiding the matches! Now he's doing spooky-looking men with long feet and holes for eyes. At least they're all smiling. He's probably seen them in a comic. When I asked him who they were he said, 'My ghosts.' 'Where do they live?' I asked.

He laughed and laughed at that. 'You know! You know!' he said.

He's very excited about meeting you. I think he's pleased that I've got a big sister just like he's got a big sister. Every now and then he gets upset and says, 'Natalie will miss me! Poor Natalie!' We should tell her, I say, then she'll know where you are and she won't worry. But that won't do either. It has to be a secret. Of course, her mother will tell her so it's not as if we're really keeping her in the dark.

This is anything but the quick note I said it was going to be. But there, I've told you all my news so I'll be able to listen to all yours.

We should arrive about five-ish on Friday. Tell Derek I'll deliver the paintings straight to the studio.

All love,
Hugo

P.S. Could you fix up a bed for Philip in my room – in case he's frightened in a strange house? And he's very fond of sausages. And doughnuts.

Philip's Dreams

Philip has two kinds of dream. His sleeping dreams and his waking dreams. Sometimes he's not quite sure which is which. In his sleeping dreams the men who come to see his ma and the Nasty Men that Natalie goes on about appear in different forms. It is a bit like a game of *Misfits.* Sometimes, for instance, the head of Dodgy Doug connects to the tattooed arms of the sailor who comes on a Friday. The Nasty Men go marching, marching, marching. Philip has no idea why they do this, but that's how it is in these dreams that are mostly nightmares, the Nasty Men marching, marching among Ma's men who all seem huge and who leer down at him and threaten to smother him. Natalie is going to get rid of the Nasty Men, and he, Philip, is going to help her.

The waking dreams are quite different and Philip would probably not call them dreams at all. Philip doesn't think in words. He thinks in pictures. This is why he feels at home with the artist. For Philip, the waking dreams are more like a place he goes to. He couldn't tell you how he gets there – only that that's where he most likes to be. Even when what he sees is scary – like the fires he sometimes sees – it is more like watching a film. He is not in it. Or if he is in it, it is impossible to see himself. As impossible as seeing yourself from the back unless you have a mirror.

Maybe it is a kindness that he can't see himself. Hugo says he once knew someone who could see into the past and the future for other people but not for herself. She had a gift, Hugo says, and he looks at Philip queerly when he says this. But Philip doesn't know what he's talking about. He doesn't know about past and future. It's all one to him. Like a continuously running film. He likes it that way. Sometimes it's funny seeing Hugo as he was when he was a little boy, even though it seems to be sad because there's another child who can't escape. Philip knows how that must feel because often he would like to escape from his ma. Sometimes even from Natalie, though he loves Natalie and just now feels sorry for her – but he won't tell her this, because Natalie hates people being sorry for her.

Philip doesn't know about the kind of fit or trance he goes into when he's Seeing. That's just the shift from the waking world to the dreaming world. To Philip it's like walking through a door. He doesn't choose to go there. It just happens.

When Hugo talks about his painting, he says that any kind of gift needs practice and looking after. 'Then you get better at it,' Hugo says, and usually he ruffles Philip's hair.

Philip has some faraway idea of what Hugo is talking about. It occurs to him that perhaps what he sees matters. Matters more than just getting rid of the Nasty Men. Philip thinks he will try to see something beautiful. And happy.

Chapter 16

Caterpillars

Can love just turn upside down into hate? I didn't know what was happening to Natalie. It was as if a whirlwind of rage was building up inside her and she couldn't stop it. She couldn't stop feeding it, turning everything into hate. Once when I was out with Lal and Paul, helping them to choose stuff for their new flat, we saw a gang of big boys kicking a smaller boy. Paul stopped them. 'People who've been hurt always seem to need to hurt someone else,' he said. It stuck in my mind that, because it made me think of Natalie. Not that it was any help. She was moving further and further away from me to some place where I couldn't reach her.

I couldn't believe it when she agreed to Hugo painting her.

'Well, why not?' she asked. I'd found her in the new coffee bar she'd taken a fancy to. It was called The Rendezvous. It had a hissing espresso machine, a juke box and a plastic rainbow curtain over the front door. Mum had told me not to go there because it was full of teddy boys. Natalie was perched on a stool. She was wearing a tight skirt with a wasp waist belt and she'd got big flowery clip-on earrings. There was a long mirror above the counter. Sitting on the stool next to Natalie's, I looked like a kid.

'Because you hate him,' I said. 'Because you keep calling him a second-rate artist. Because you stole some of his things – paintings, drawings . . .'

'Me?' Natalie opened her eyes wide. 'I don't give a toss about Hugo,' she said, 'so why would I do that?'

'Because he's taken Philip over. Because you don't think he's safe. Because you were angry. Because, because, because . . .' I didn't dare risk *because you think he's a LON*. Why put an idea in her head if it wasn't already there?

'I was angry,' she agreed easily. 'But there's no need. Philip's still Seeing. At night now. More of the dream visions.' Was she lying? Was she telling the truth? I no longer knew.

She was so calm and distant that somehow I felt it was more scary than when she lost her temper. There was something thrilling about Natalie when she lost her temper, something that had made me love her. The passion, I suppose. I couldn't quite believe or trust this new mood of lofty calm. And I was bothered by the news of Philip's dreams. I thought he'd been too happy with Hugo to have any of the awful kind.

'What?' I asked. 'What's he been dreaming . . . I mean, Seeing?'

'I haven't quite worked it out yet,' said Natalie. 'You know . . . translated.'

I didn't want to be reminded of translating. The last time we'd talked in that way, Philip's dream had been 'translated' into Mr Oliver as a Left-Over Nazi.

'I'll let you know,' Natalie said, then, 'Oops! I almost forgot. You've chickened out, haven't you?'

I could feel myself blushing. 'I wouldn't call it that,' I said.

'Anyway, I don't need to bother about Hugo,' Natalie said airily and as if she'd never gone on and on about him bribing Philip.

I stirred the froth on my coffee. I was glad the windows of the coffee bar were steamed up so that Mum wouldn't see me if she went past. We shared the place with two teddy boys – slick quiffed hair, long jackets, shoestring ties. They looked Natalie and me over and laughed together.

Natalie played with her hair and made pouting faces in the long mirror. 'I quite fancy being painted,' she said. 'What d'you think I should wear for my portrait?'

'Wear your birthday suit, love,' one of the teddy boys called over.

Natalie ignored him.

'I don't care,' I said. 'I don't care what you wear!'

I slid off the stool and paid for my coffee.

Natalie laughed. 'Going already?' she said. 'I wonder, did you want Hugo all to yourself? Poor Lizzie. You're not exactly an artist's dream boat, are you?'

I didn't answer her. I pushed my way out through the rainbow curtain. This was her revenge, I thought. Revenge for the day on the beach when I'd stayed put, chosen Hugo instead of going with her. Did Natalie never forgive anyone anything? And the worst of it was that I could completely understand why Hugo wanted to paint her. If I was Hugo, I'd have felt the same way. Shelley's *Wild Spirit*, my kindred spirit. As she'd been. As she wasn't any more.

Perhaps I should have stayed away when Natalie posed for Hugo, but I couldn't. What was I hoping? That he'd get fed up with her? That she wouldn't come? On the first morning she drifted up the beach wearing a dress I'd never seen before. It made her look about twenty. She'd put on lipstick and more of the weighty mascara. I remembered all the materials I'd seen in her bedroom. I remembered her strutting about in the old coat with swastikas drawn on the lining like someone out of a film about the French Resistance. I remembered her first appearance at school, the way she made even a gymslip look sexy. Could Natalie play any part she wanted? This time she'd dressed herself as the artist's muse. She was all drapes and mystery, her hair let loose in a wild tangle, the dress slipping off one shoulder.

If Hugo was surprised or amused, he hid it. Nor did he laugh at her this time. He fell into the role she wanted. He played 'artist', arranging a chair for her with a shawl flung over the back of it. He got her to turn this way and that to show her left profile, then her right. The dress was silky. Natalie slid off her shoes and allowed the dress to slip up her thighs. Hugo drew. Every now and again he'd shout, 'Keep still!' because Natalie seemed determined to look in every corner of the caravan so that I wondered if she was planning another raid. More sketchbooks. More paintings. Surely now that Hugo was doing her portrait she'd give up?

'OK, OK,' she'd say, and move easily back into her pose. 'Keep your hair on, Mr Artist.'

Philip clambered up to the bunk bed and fell asleep. I sat on the caravan step and watched. Miserably. Hugo seemed to have forgotten his drawings of me entirely. I could hardly blame him. Natalie's looks were exotic. Mine, dull. Ordinary, English and dull.

Of course Natalie wanted to see the portrait as it proceeded. Hugo refused. Natalie sulked. 'If you were a proper artist,' she said, hands on hips, still posing in the light from the caravan's open door, 'you'd pay your models. That's what artists do. Even the very poor ones. I've read about it.'

'Maybe I'm not a proper artist,' said Hugo. 'You don't need to come back if you don't want to. I've plenty of other work. And Lizzie and Philip to draw.'

'I might. I might not,' said Natalie with a shrug.

'Please yourself,' said Hugo. They were equally stubborn, Hugo and Natalie. Both intense. Both passionate. But going in opposite directions – Hugo to the light, Natalie to the dark – or that's how it seemed that week when Natalie was all charm on the outside and all rage on the inside.

'Dangerous!' said Hugo, watching her walk away without a backward glance.

'Is that what you like about her?' Despite myself, my voice sounded wistful.

Hugo ruffled my hair. 'Aspects of childhood. That's what interests me. Natalie's just leaving it. Childhood, I mean. It's like caterpillar to butterfly. Catching her between . . . How about you go paddling now and I'll do some more sketches.'

I did as he asked even though I didn't want to be 'an aspect of childhood' and I felt a long way off butterfly.

Hugo followed me down the beach with his sketchpad. It was one of those warm but windy afternoons when the sea is quite rough and the waves come in at you with a great grabbing rush and the sun seems to be joining in the game. I liked the feeling of the salty wind blowing through my T-shirt, and having to jump back when a large wave came. For a few moments – minutes only – I almost forgot about Hugo sketching. When I looked back at him, I saw he was smiling and knew that that was just what he wanted. Me forgetting myself. Then suddenly I found myself crying. It was as if Hugo had seen me naked, or seen the inside of me, or seen something that was just me and private, private, private.

And Hugo seemed to understand because he put his arms round

me and hugged me. He smelled of paint and sea salt and sweat and I wanted to just stay there, in his arms for ever.

Philip had woken up. He came hopping down the beach and wound his arms round both of us. Hugo laughed. Let go of me and lifted Philip up.

'Philip and I are going to London, aren't we, old chap? I'm taking some of the paintings for the exhibition. I'll take a second batch later. And I'm going to show Philip the sights.'

'The p-p-palace and the t-t-tower . . .' said Philip.

'And all the bridges,' said Hugo.

'Does Natalie know?' I asked.

Both Hugo and Philip suddenly looked sheepish.

'Well, I expect Mrs Rafferty will tell her,' said Hugo.

'M-M-Ma will tell,' Philip echoed.

'Want to see the portrait so far?' Hugo asked.

We went back into the caravan. Hugo had covered the portrait with an old sheet. He lifted it off.

I just stood and stared at it.

'Well?' Hugo asked. 'Well?'

I saw that he'd scribbled a title for the portrait. It was 'Angry Girl'.

But the Natalie of Hugo's portrait was half girl and half bird of prey. I suppose you could see a kind of beauty in it, a wildness, the colours you might find in a butterfly – maybe a Red Admiral, all reds and blacks – but what dominated the portrait was the rage he'd caught. I remembered how Natalie had said Philip could see the swastika on someone's heart. Hugo had seen the rage in Natalie's.

'There's nothing I can do,' Hugo said. 'I have to paint what I see. That's what I saw.'

'She'll hate it,' I said.

Natalie's Diary

Midnight, Monday

He's made me so ugly! Maybe I am that ugly. I can't look in the mirror any more. This morning when I looked it was as if I was looking at the painting. His horrible, horrible painting.

It was easy getting in the caravan. I just busted the door. And I'm glad. Glad I did it. Glad I got in and knifed that painting. Stabbed it and stabbed it. I wished I was stabbing him. I wished I was stabbing all Ma's men but mostly him, Mr Artist. If I hadn't done it he'd have taken me away and shown me in galleries and places. People looking at me, saying, *Who's that ugly girl?*

It wasn't enough that he'd stolen Philip. How could Ma let him go off like that? We had a fight. I called her a bitch. She slapped my face. I could hide my face for ever. I stabbed it and stabbed it. I used one of his knives.

Lizzie's soft on him. Moony. I can't trust her any more. Can't call her my kindred spirit. She's betrayed me. They all betray me, but him worst of all. Mr Artist. Mr Left-Over Nazi. He called the painting 'Angry Girl'. I'll show him angry.

Philip will forget him. It'll be easy. He'll go away at the end of the summer. Ha ha ha for Lizzie! What do I care if she breaks her heart?

I'll make sure he never comes back to Norton. Never. Never. Never.

Maybe I'll do it on the day Lizzie's a bridesmaid. *See this,* I'll say. *This is Mr Artist's angry girl. And bye-bye, lover boy.*

Note to Self. Keep watch.

Chapter 17
Bridesmaids

The day of the wedding, I looked at myself in my bridesmaid's dress and wanted to run away. I should have looked pretty. Even if I didn't want Lal leaving home, the wedding was about love. I should have looked happy. The dress was pretty enough. It was my face – me inside it – that didn't.

'What's happened to you this summer?' Mum asked, coming into my bedroom to see how I was getting on. She was already in her wedding gear – silky grey dress with little beads across the front, and a feathery hat. I thought she must have been very pretty when she was a girl. 'You look as if the spark's gone out of you. Even your hair looks limp,' she said. She tried to fluff it up with the brush and failed. Together we looked at me in the mirror.

'Smile!' said Mum.

I smiled.

Mum gave me a hug. 'Think of it as getting a brother,' she said.

'I know,' I said. 'I like him.' Actually, I was surprised to find that I did.

'Well, then,' said Mum, 'that's happy ever after, isn't it? There's nothing else worrying you, is there, Lizzie?'

I shook my head. How could I begin? How could I get through this wedding when I couldn't stop going over and over the awful moment when I'd found Natalie in Hugo's caravan? I couldn't sleep for the scene re-playing in my head.

I knew Hugo had gone to London. Saw the door of the caravan open. Found Natalie inside. She'd slashed the portrait of her on the easel with what looked like a bread knife. Now she was ripping pages out of the sketchbooks, had pulled out some canvases Hugo had left to take later and was about to slash those too.

'What are you doing?' I shrieked at her.

She turned on me then. All the wildness that had once meant a kind of freedom now turned into a terrible hate.

'He's got Philip,' she said. She stabbed the portrait one last time. 'And he did this to me.'

'He'll bring Philip back,' I said. I wanted to be fierce, strong, stop her doing any more damage, but the tears were running down my face and I couldn't stop shaking.

'You think he's so good, your Mr Artist,' Natalie sneered. 'But I know what he's really about. You'll see. When it's over, you'll see!'

'Hugo's only about painting!' I said. 'That's all he cares about.'

I saw then that she'd got a bag with her. She'd found the early drawings Hugo had done of Philip. They included one I knew Hugo was proud of, a drawing of Philip wearing a seaweed crown and looking like a mermaid's child. And she'd found the preliminary drawings Hugo had done of her, almost cartoons that made her look half eagle, half girl.

'I'm taking what's mine,' Natalie said. 'Philip's mine. He'll know what Mr Artist's really like. I'll show him. Philip can't survive without me. He'll always need me.'

'Give me the bag,' I said. 'Let me put things back. It's not too late. Please!'

Natalie laughed in my face. Laughed hysterically. 'Poor Lizzie,' she said. 'Poor little rich girl! Remind me never to think of you as a friend ever again.'

Then she was off, slinging the bag over her shoulder as if it weighed nothing, though it was full of drawings, and I watched her cross the beach, barefoot, her hair wild as a tangle of snakes. Still with the strut in her walk.

I wished there was some way I could warn Hugo before he got back to Norton, but there wasn't. All I could do was hang about the caravan on the off-chance of seeing his battered old Rover come down the sea road. And I was lucky, if you can call it lucky to be the one to break bad news. I saw them arriving. The pair of them looked so happy. I saw Philip giving Hugo a final hug before Hugo patted his bum and sent him limping and running home.

I stood by the caravan door, unable to speak. Hugo took one look at my face and said, 'Natalie!'

'I'm sorry,' I said. 'I couldn't stop her.' I think I was wringing my hands. I've read about people doing that. I never expected to do it myself.

Without a word Hugo went into the caravan. The lock had been broken but otherwise there was enough of the door for him to close it behind him. I sat on the sand, waiting, listening to him moving about inside. Sometimes I heard him groan. Once there was a kind of howl of rage. I guessed it was the loss of the picture of Philip as a mermaid's child.

There was nothing I could do, but I sat on, wanting to comfort him, wanting to try and explain.

When he did come out, it was as if his hair had suddenly turned an even sharper red, but that was because his face had gone so white. His hands were shaking. He was holding the slashed portrait of Natalie and broke it across his knee.

'Go home, Lizzie,' he said. 'Go home and find a new friend.'

'There's things you should know . . .' I began. I wanted to tell him all about Natalie's idea that evil couldn't just end, that there were Left-Over Nazis hiding everywhere, that we'd hunted down Mr Oliver. I wanted to confess. I wanted to feel clean and free again. I wanted to start afresh.

But Hugo didn't want to know.

'She's ill, your Natalie,' he said. 'Wounded. It happens to some children. And sometimes there's nothing you can do to make it better.'

He sounded so terribly sad that I wanted to hug him as Philip had done, but he turned away. 'Go home, Lizzie,' he repeated. 'I've got some rescuing to do.'

'I'll come and help,' I said. 'Tomorrow. I can come and tidy. Maybe I can put some of the sketchbooks together – the pages that aren't torn.'

Hugo ruffled my hair. 'Come tomorrow if you want,' he said.

I'd never told him about the wedding, about Lal and Paul, about how life was in our house. My time with Hugo, my heart time / art time, was separate, special – almost a world in itself with just him and me and the paintings and drawings. So I didn't tell him now that it wasn't easy to get away from the house because the wedding was the next day, and Mum and Lal had me running a hundred and one errands. *Take this. Do that. Make tea. Phone the hairdresser.*

When I did manage to escape, it was late in the morning and I found Hugo packing canvases into the Rover. The caravan itself never went up to London with him. All winter it was kept in a garage owned by Mrs Kipper, the fish-cart woman. Hugo always said the caravan was too old for the journey. So was the Rover by the look of it. But it had a large boot and a roof rack. I saw that Hugo had already fixed a new lock on the caravan door.

'It's not time yet!' I said. 'You always stay until the end of September. That's just before my birthday.'

'I can't risk any more paintings being destroyed,' Hugo said. 'I've an exhibition coming up. I'm going to take these up to London, then I'll come back for a couple of days. Clear the caravan. Put it to bed for the winter, as it were.'

'I'll see you before you go?' I said.

'Course you will.'

'You could try and get Philip to bring back the sketchbooks she's taken,' I said. I could hardly bring myself to use Natalie's name.

'I don't think I want to make things worse for Philip,' said Hugo.

How could we have guessed?

And it wasn't Philip I was thinking of on the morning of the wedding. It was just Hugo. How I was going to miss him. How I'd only just begun learning to draw. Learning to draw and learning to love.

I looked in the mirror at my bridesmaid self and tried to smile.

Lal put her head round my door. 'Could you try not to look quite so heartbroken,' she said. 'It's not as if you'll never see me again.'

Philip's Dreams

Philip is happy snugged up in the bunk bed of the caravan. He has run away from Natalie although she doesn't know it yet. He has a very full tin of biscuits that might last him all the time that Hugo is away. Hugo has given him the new key to the caravan but he is to keep it hidden. Particularly from Natalie. *I don't think your sister likes me much, old chap.*

Philip knows that this is true and though he loves Natalie and will always love her because she is the sister who has always looked after him, he doesn't much like her at the moment because she is so angry all the time and because she has torn up pages of Hugo's drawings.

Philip is going to stay in the caravan. He is going to eat all the biscuits and he is going to draw a picture of Hugo's sister who looked after him when he was in London and who is the prettiest person Philip has ever seen. Philip dreams that one day he will live with Hugo and Helena.

He dreams of a horse that pulls the caravan along as if it is now a gypsy caravan and the three of them are gypsies. The caravan has grown. It is big enough for all of them. He'll keep some of the biscuits for when Hugo and Helena come home.

Curled up in the bunk he can hear some distant music and laughter. The music weaves itself into his dream as if there are people dancing. Even his ma. Even Natalie. All of them dancing.

Chapter 18
The Yellow Caravan

It was afternoon by the time the dancing began. Dad had chosen the Hotel Victoria for the wedding reception. He'd wanted somewhere grand. Somewhere that would show we'd come up in the world, had money, success. He'd looked at umpteen hotels trying to find the right one. A hotel grand enough. The Hotel Victoria was it. It had grand pillars at the entrance. You went into a hall that was all dark mahogany, hushed carpets, big vases of gladioli or maybe roses. Waiters slid past you on soft feet, balancing trays on one hand.

What won Dad over completely was the ballroom. You came down from the dining room into a room where Cinderella herself might have danced beneath the glittering candlelight of an enormous chandelier that hung from the centre. There were dainty gilt chairs and small tables for people who weren't dancing to sit at, a small stage – presumably for a band – and, best of all, one wall entirely made up of windows looking out at the sea. Somehow the hotel had acquired its own small, private beach. Doors opened up from it so that on a hot day, guests could drift outside and be served cool drinks.

When Dad had first considered the Hotel Victoria, the hotel

manager had taken us down to the ballroom and swept open the glass doors onto the beach. 'Yes!' Dad said, and, 'Yes!' And then I cringed while he told the manager a long story about his son-in-law-to-be being in the navy and therefore a wedding reception overlooking the sea had exactly the right atmosphere, and of course we planned on a small orchestra and no expense was to be spared, et cetera, et cetera, until I wandered back up to the entrance hall, pretending I wasn't with him.

The church was only round the corner from the Hotel Victoria but we still had to be taken there in flower-filled cars because Dad said it would look silly to walk, so there were Lal and Paul, looking all pinkly radiant, in one car, and me and Paul's little cousin Gemma (bridesmaid two) in another car.

The nice part – the church part with Paul waiting at the altar for Lal and Lal looking beautiful, then the hymns, then coming out to everyone throwing confetti – that was over. I'd seen Alice and Dottie outside the church. I'd smiled at them and they'd smiled back. All that kind of numbed the ache in my heart that couldn't stop thinking of Hugo. Hugo leaving. Summer ending. Natalie – Natalie, lost.

But then there was all the greeting of guests and people telling me how sweet Gemma and I looked, and how old was I now. I'd taken off the childish rosebud Alice band as soon as the photographer had finished. Then there was a very long and boring lunch to get through. How many courses does one person need? The speeches seemed longer still. By then there was nothing to dull the ache. If anything, the music for the dancing made it worse.

It was from the window of the ballroom that I suddenly realized I could see Hugo's caravan. *Dear yellow caravan,* I thought. *Dear cheery yellow caravan!*

The band struck up the first waltz. Lal and Paul took to the floor. 'What a lovely young couple,' I heard one of the guests saying.

'And so much in love,' answered her friend.

Here and there along the windowsill of the ballroom the hotel had provided binoculars. They were there, I supposed, so you could view the birds or maybe the islands far out beyond the pier. Idly, and because no one was likely to ask me to dance, I picked up a pair and looked towards the caravan.

There was only one figure on the beach and as I focused the binoculars I realized it was Natalie. It took me a few moments to work out what she was doing. Even when I realized she was making a bonfire – adding to the driftwood Hugo kept by piling on old fishboxes and any piece of wood she could find – I didn't understand her intention. It was only when I saw the flames leaping up, saw how close they were to the caravan, that I realized what she was up to.

I couldn't believe my eyes. Forgetting all the wedding guests, I hitched up my dress and climbed up onto one of the fragile gilt chairs. What I saw with the binoculars pressed to my eyes made me so dizzy I thought I was going to faint. The caravan stood with its front door facing Natalie. The back of it, where the bunk beds were kept, faced me. And there, at the window, as the flames licked at the yellow paint like so many hungry tongues, I saw a face. Philip's.

Although I couldn't hear him, I could see that he was hammering on the window with his fists. I knew by the way Natalie was dancing about, throwing wood on the fire, that she hadn't seen him and had no idea he was in there. How could she? From where she was she couldn't see him. As for Philip, either total panic, the smoke – or both – held him trapped where he was. He appeared unable to move, to reach the door, to escape. Seeing, but not hearing, his fists on the window was like him screaming for help and no sound coming out. I could see but not hear; Natalie couldn't do either. The noise of the fire would have blocked out his cries. That or the madness in her head.

I knew what had happened. Hugo, to comfort Philip, had given him a key to the caravan and Philip, missing Hugo, would have gone to the caravan, curled up in the bunk bed and fallen asleep.

'What are you doing, Little Sis? Come and dance with me.' It was Paul, lifting me down from the chair – only now I was screaming at him. Screaming so loud that even the band stopped playing and the guests froze as if they were all in that party game of statues.

'The boy! There's a boy in the caravan! On fire! It's Philip! We've got to save him!' I think that's what I was screaming, all the time dragging Paul outside. Maybe being in the navy made Paul know how to act fast in an emergency. He flung off his black wedding tails, lifted me over the fence that sheltered the hotel's private beach garden and together we raced across the sand to the caravan. I remember Paul seemed to be scattering clothes as we ran. His tie, his shoes, his waistcoat.

It was late afternoon by now. There was Natalie. A small black figure turned into a silhouette by the brightness of the fire. She was dancing, dancing goblin-like, barefoot, her hair as wild as a tangle of seaweed. I ran towards her screaming, 'What are you doing? What are you doing? Philip's in there! Philip!'

She seemed deaf to my screams. Deaf to reason. I saw the flash of her teeth and knew she was smiling. She was working hard, dancing about the fire, gathering more and more wood. Her whole figure expressed triumph as she flung a last piece of driftwood at the caravan. The paintwork, the sunshine yellow, was crackling and blistering as though it had caught not fire but some awful skin disease. There was probably no need for the can of petrol Natalie had obviously brought with her. Hugo's turps and oils and the canister of calor gas he kept inside the caravan would have been enough.

Natalie seemed to be dancing about the beach like a whirling dervish when I grabbed hold of her. Paul had rushed at the caravan and was trying to pull open the door. Either the fire had sealed it or Philip had locked it. Locked it to keep Natalie out. He was more successful than he ever could have imagined.

'Philip!' I bawled in Natalie's ear. 'Philip's in there!'

She stopped dead in her tracks. 'No!' she howled. 'No!' And it was a wolf howl, a howl of agony. 'I left him at home. He's at home. I shut him in. I shut him in!'

I dragged her to the back of the caravan. Both of us could see his face now. And we could see the key hung round his neck, could see him trying to pull it free of the string and failing. We could see the lenses of his specs clouding up. Then he dropped away from the window. I ran back to Paul at the caravan's door. Paul's face, his shirt, his hands, were blackened by the fire. My bridesmaid dress caught on the instant. Paul turned and ripped it from me. Together we hurled ourselves at the door. But somehow Natalie crawled under us, was there when the door exploded outwards. I saw the flames licking at her hair, her legs, her shorts and I flung myself beside her, grabbing her ankles, trying and failing to pull her out. It was like the first time we'd crawled into the dark of the air-raid shelter, only now she was crawling into a mouth of fire.

It was Paul who dragged Philip's body out. The pair of us fell together onto the beach. Almost the last thing I can remember before there was an ambulance man fitting an oxygen mask on my face was Lal running down the beach in her wedding dress, the guests coming after her.

Natalie was still howling, 'Not him! Not Philip!' when the fire engine arrived and one of the firemen hauled her out, her hair ablaze, her face, arms, legs blackened, her burned face streaked by tears. He tried to prevent her from seeing Philip, lying there clutching a few shreds of one of Hugo's old jerseys. His T-shirt – a new one Hugo had bought for him – had been burned away. The fire had done what he couldn't – freed the key from its string. Natalie flung up her arms to try and reach him, hold him, keep him, then she lost consciousness. The ambulance men put her on a stretcher, wrapped Philip's body in some kind of cloth and took both of them away, the siren echoing up the beach as if it had taken over Natalie's howl.

The rest of the day and night is a jumble. I remember Dad saying, 'Well, at least everyone got to eat the wedding breakfast.' I remember Lal and Paul weeping in each other's arms. I remember my badly burned hands and Mum calling in Dr Janie, who cooed over them and bandaged them into paws and gave me something to help me sleep. It didn't help much. I remember I spent all the night tossing and turning and all the time I was thinking, *How can I tell Hugo? How can I tell him?*

Of course, I didn't have to tell Hugo. There were plenty of others to do it. It turned out that he had more friends in Norton than I could have guessed. People he'd sketched or painted. Mrs Kipper of the fish cart, at least two of our teachers, Mr Smithers from the library. Hugo had been a kind of summer fixture in Norton and so when he came back from London and found his caravan destroyed, people rallied round, told him about Philip, offered him tea or supper, a bed for the night. Somehow I think Hugo had come to *mean* summer to the people of Norton and they'd come to love him for it.

As for me, I missed the first week of the autumn term. Lal and Paul said I could come and stay with them any time I wanted, but I was too shaky. There were still the nightmares in which the fire was eating up the whole beach, roaring so fiercely that even the sea couldn't put it out. And Philip was in the middle, holding a bunch of paintbrushes like a bouquet of flowers. Sometimes Hugo was there. Sometimes Lal and Paul in their wedding clothes. The fire never touches them.

The shakes and the nightmares and the pills went on for weeks. The worst of the nightmares were when I seemed to change into Natalie. We weren't just kindred spirits, we were one person. It was as if love, hate and Philip's death had bonded us and I could never be just me again.

If it hadn't been for Lal and Paul, maybe I'd never have recovered. They were the only people I told about the hunt for the Left-Over Nazis, about Natalie seeing darkness and evil everywhere, about Philip's Seeing and Hugo's art. They let me rant on for hours until I'd exhausted it all, until I was ready not to forget – that was impossible – but to pick up my life again. As me.

Epilogue

Apart from Lal and Paul, no one ever knew what Natalie and I had done. About our quest for Left-Over Nazis, our persecution of Sam, Maisie and Mr Oliver, because we never told. The burning of the caravan was put down to an accident, a child playing with fire. Hugo could have got on to the police, of course, but he'd rescued his paintings. He'd been too late to rescue Philip.

Maybe now that I've told this story, the guilt I've felt for so long will fade. Often I've thought that of the two of us, I was guiltier than Natalie. There was so much that drove Natalie – poverty, the death of her father, the awful 'uncles', her alcoholic mother. Over and over again I've asked myself what we shared, what made us 'kindred spirits'. Was it simply that we were both war-babies, the stories of the war working on our psyches like a blight? I've read that in 1939, during the Phoney War, everyone imagined there were German spies everywhere. For us, the fifties seemed to be a phoney peace. So although it was Natalie who lit the fire, Natalie who caused Philip's death, my failure was not seeing what the uncles were doing to her, not seeing how much she needed me, not seeing how Philip was her only anchor, not seeing how much Hugo's portrait of her hurt. Not seeing!

And maybe in the end that was what that summer was all about – ways of seeing. Natalie seeing darkness, evil everywhere, Philip with a Seer's gift, Hugo painting the sea, the sky, children like us.

Almost all Hugo's paintings – and no, he wasn't a great painter, just a good man trying to see – looked into the distance as if he was always seeing possibilities: the space of sea and sky, the future, hope.

Mrs Rafferty left Norton after Philip's death and Natalie was, as she put it, 'taken away' – by which she meant taken to a children's home. I've no idea where Mrs Rafferty went or if the 'uncles' went with her or if, as is more likely, she found new ones. Nor do I know where Natalie is now, though sometimes I run a fantasy about seeking her out, the two of us meeting over coffee or a bottle of wine, forgiving each other, laughing, finding our kindred spirit selves again. But I don't do it.

Hugo never came back to Norton again. Some months after the fire he sent me three portraits he'd done of me and one of Philip. There was no address on the package and although I look through all the brochures from the art galleries I never find any news of him. Maybe he went abroad. Maybe he has another yellow caravan on another beach. I hope so. I keep his paintings on the wall of my studio.

Apart from being an artist now, perhaps more importantly, I'm also an auntie. Lal and Paul's little boy, Jake, often comes to stay with me. When I watch him playing I wonder how many generations it takes for the memory of war not to touch a child's mind and I hope it hasn't touched Jake.

I try to paint him. Sometimes I take my paints and easel onto the beach. I pack a picnic for Jake. I watch him and paint. I try to really see. I try to do what Hugo taught me to do – to catch the light.